PEPPERMINT PERIL

A CUPCAKE CRIMES MYSTERY

MOLLY MAPLE

MARY E. TWOMEY, LLC

PEPPERMINT PERIL

Book Five in the Cupcake Crimes Series

By

Molly Maple

COPYRIGHT

Copyright © 2021 Mary E. Twomey LLC
Cover Art by Emcat Designs

All rights reserved.
First Edition: June 2021

This is a work of fiction. Any resemblance of characters to actual persons, living or dead, is purely coincidental. The author holds exclusive rights to this work. Unauthorized duplication is prohibited.

This book is licensed for your personal enjoyment only. If you would like to share this book with another person, please purchase an additional copy for each reader. Thank you for respecting the hard work of this author.

For information:
http://www.MollyMapleMysteries.com

DEDICATION

To my parents,

Who treat the childhood Christmas ornaments we made in haste as if they are pure gold.

ABOUT PEPPERMINT PERIL

When a packed Christmas party turns into a murder scene, the small town of Sweetwater Falls has no shortage of suspects.

When Charlotte McKay uncovers a body while catering a Christmas party, she doesn't know who she can trust. The people who hired her are quick to point the finger in her direction, ramping up her need to find the real criminal. But everywhere she turns, there is a new suspect, and another lie she has to sift through to get to the truth.

Charlotte doesn't believe that the couple who plays Santa and Mrs. Claus every year at the Christmas festival is capable of something as dastardly as murder, but Nick and Nancy's alibi turns up one lie after another. Sweetwater Falls has a bounty of wholesome, wonderful people, but the more Charlotte digs for the truth, she begins to uncover secrets that are best left in the dark.

Charlotte knows she needs to find the murderer fast, but when no one is willing to tell the whole truth, Charlotte is afraid she will be brought in for a crime she didn't commit.

"Peppermint Peril" is filled with layered clues and cozy moments, written by Molly Maple, which is a pen name for a USA Today bestselling author.

1

CHRISTMAS CATERING

I have never been more stressed in my life. Or if I have, I cannot recall it, nor do I want to relive anything close to the anxiety that causes this pounding in my chest. Sweat runs down my spine as I pick up the box of cupcakes, praying none of them tipped or tilted on the drive. I was so careful, going well below the meager speed limit and taking each turn with care as if I were transporting an unbuckled newborn.

This is why I make people pick up their cupcakes. The Bravery Bakery has been my sole source of income for almost a month now. Generally, I feel like I've got the hang of things, except for last week, when Nick and Nancy asked if they could pay extra for me to deliver their order. I said yes without thinking of how stressful it is to drive baked goods from one home to another.

"It's going to be fine," Marianne tells me from her spot

in the passenger seat of my red sedan. "Not one person has complained that when they took their cupcakes home, everything was smashed to pieces."

All I take out of my best friend's assurance is the visual of my hours of hard work being smashed to pieces inside the delivery boxes.

Marianne grimaces. "That was supposed to make you feel better, but I think you just turned paler."

"This is my first catering job. If I screw this up, it will be my only catering job."

Marianne turns her head so the meager winter sun can shine on her olive skin through the window. "I'm right here, Charlotte McKay. Nothing bad is going to happen to those desserts."

I park the car on the street in front of Nick and Nancy's sizable colonial. I'm last in the row of four other cars parked along the curb in front of their house.

Marianne points to a blue sedan with a cracked back window taking up space in the driveway. "I wish we could park closer to the house. That would make things easier."

"Meh. I don't want to get boxed in." Though I see a shadowy figure trotting out of the side of the house and getting into the car to leave, I don't want to take that spot, for fear of someone coming in behind me and blocking me in the driveway. Even when the blue car pulls away, I don't take the spot, but turn off my engine and draw in a steadying breath.

I gape at the pretty white shutters set against the stately

brick. Leading up to the house are a dozen small, well-trimmed bushes shaped to look like Christmas trees, complete with blue and white twinkling lights. There are candles in every window, and an enormous Christmas wreath on the front door.

Though the white-haired couple seemed sweet and unassuming when they booked the job with me, I can see they have expensive taste and put thought into the details.

My stomach sinks. "Oh my goodness. I put sprinkles on the peppermint cupcakes."

Marianne tilts her head at me, her chin-length chestnut hair swinging to the side. "Red and green sprinkles. What's wrong with that? I think they're cute."

I shake my head with plenty of self-loathing flooding my system, suddenly regretting my choices that seemed fitting at the time. "No, no, no. It's all wrong. They like things expensive and upscale. Red and green sprinkles are fun and festive. My design is all wrong." I pinch the bridge of my nose. "It's going to look cheap against the backdrop of all this." I motion to the perfect house that looks like it should be featured on a Christmas card.

Marianne reaches across the console and squeezes my hand. "You're freaking out. It's going to be just fine. Nick and Nancy are fun people. Nick plays Santa Claus at the Christmas Festival every year, and Nancy is Mrs. Claus. Don't let the house intimidate you."

I lean my head against the back of my seat. "We are

never catering again. This is so stressful. I'm going to ruin their party."

I don't expect Marianne to chuckle at me, but the sound adds a little levity to my certain doom. "If cupcakes can make or break a party, then it's a pretty boring affair, isn't it. Let's go, Charlotte. You'll see there's nothing to worry about."

I take my time getting out of the car, steeling myself for the worst-case scenario.

The cupcakes are smashed to pieces.

The cookies have crumbled.

The donuts have staled and cracked.

I suck in a deep breath when I open my trunk, hoping I haven't screwed up my first catering gig. I pop open the lid of the box, heaving a sigh of relief when I see none of the cupcakes have tilted.

Marianne grabs up two boxes of desserts, scolding me as we walk our baked goods to the house. "You are going to give yourself an ulcer, worrying like this. Desserts are fun. Enjoy the ride, Charlotte the Brave. You've got this."

Without Marianne, I would be nothing close to calm.

When I knock on the side door (the front door is for guests, the side door is for the help, I was told over the phone) and am greeted by Nancy, relief floods my features.

The plump woman with pinned white hair and minimal makeup is dressed as Mrs. Claus, complete with an apron lined with candy canes. She lights up at the sight of us. "Oh, perfect timing! I thought I heard you in the kitchen just a minute ago. That wasn't you?" She doesn't pause for our answer. "I told everyone the dinner started at five o'clock, but a handful of people showed up early to get a peek at the decorations. They've gone through most of my hors d'oeuvres already. They can snack on your cookies while we wait for the rest of the guests to arrive."

Marianne kisses Nancy on the cheek. "Where would you like us to set the desserts, Mrs. Claus?"

"Follow me to the dining area, girls." She ushers us through the huge, spotless kitchen without stopping, taking us toward a grand table laden with picked-over trays in the dining room. "Can you put the donuts and cookies here for people to eat now? We'll save the cupcakes for after dinner." She motions to a silver tray in the center. "You can use that to set the cookies and donuts on. It's almost time for the party to start."

Christmas music plays in the background, highlighting the season amid the garland and nutcrackers everywhere I look.

The doorbell rings, and Nancy throws her hands up, pleasantly exasperated. "The hostess' work is never done, it seems. Thank goodness you took over desserts this year, Charlotte. I honestly don't know what I would have done. Every year, our Christmas party gets bigger and bigger. Last year, it was thirty people. This year we are expecting fifty!" She wrings her hands as she makes her way out of the dining room. "Oh, I hope there's enough ham."

Marianne and I share a "yikes" look between us. We

begin popping open the lids on our boxes so we can fill the giant silver tray with donuts and cookies.

The cookies haven't crumbled, and the donuts haven't staled. I laugh to myself at how stressed I was over nothing. When Whiskers, Nick and Nancy's cat, saunters past us, coiling its tail around my ankle and then moving to Marianne to do the same, I finally breathe.

"You make the desserts look all pretty on the tray," Marianne instructs. "I'm going to consolidate some of these hors d'oeuvres, so it doesn't look as picked over. Sheesh, people showed up early, and her appetizers are halfway gone before the party's even started."

We work quickly and in tandem, no doubt because we have spent so much time together in the kitchen, baking and laughing in a happy rhythm while we work to make my dream of owning my own cupcakery come true.

By the time the donuts and cookies are set up, Marianne is finished making the hors d'oeuvres look fresh and well-presented. She gathers up the unused trays while I take the boxes of cupcakes, following her back to the kitchen.

Everything smells like ham and butter. My mouth waters because it is not possible to remain unaffected when an aroma this enticing enters your nose. All that is needed to complete the picture of perfection is a roaring fireplace and a plateful of cookies.

"Now don't you feel silly, worrying like you did? Nancy

is happy, and your cupcakes are amazing. Christmas is all about red and green, which you did with the sprinkles."

I smile at her as I set the cupcake boxes on the counter. All worry is leaving me, taking weight off my spine and shoulders so I stand taller, embracing every centimeter of my five-foot-ten inches. "You're right. Next time I start spiraling, I'll try to remember how much I stressed out today, and how it was all for nothing." I cast around the immaculate kitchen. "Any guesses where a clean tray might be for me to set the cupcakes out for her?"

Marianne shrugs. "Check the cupboards." She motions around the kitchen. "And for the record, my kitchen looks nothing like this when I cook for a party. Hers is perfectly clean. Mine generally looks like a culinary bomb went off if I try cooking a huge feast." She shakes her head. "I suspect Nick and Nancy actually have Christmas elves working around the house for them, cleaning when no one is looking."

I chuckle at Marianne's positing. "It's the only explanation."

She stands over the stove and inhales deeply, her eyes rolling back. "I'm warning you, if we don't get set up and get out of here soon, I'm going to open up that oven and start picking at the ham. It smells too delicious to resist."

Marianne sets the dirty trays in the dishwasher while I open cupboards to see if I can locate something on which to display my cupcakes.

"Agreed. Eating my weight in ham is all I can think

about right now. My parents and I never did big meals like that around Christmas," I tell Marianne. "We usually just got takeout."

Marianne's nose crinkles. "No offense to your childhood, but that is not happening this year. You live with Winifred now. If there is anything your great-aunt is good at, it's making a killer Christmas dinner. The Live Forever Club's cooking skills really shine around the holidays. Agnes makes the potatoes with so much butter, I could eat only that and be totally satisfied. Karen makes wassail, her green gelatin dessert and usually a side dish—again with enough butter to stop a horse's heart. Winifred makes ham with pineapples." Marianne swoons, shutting the dishwasher door. "It's heavenly."

I have no idea what wassail is, but everything else sounds delicious. "What do you make?"

"A mess, usually." Marianne chuckles at herself. "I bring a salad. It's hard to mess that up. Our Christmas dinner is always on Christmas Eve—the day after the town's big Christmas Festival. That's a whole thing of its own. You'll love it."

"I've loved every event I've been to in Sweetwater Falls so far. I have no doubt the Christmas Festival will be just as fun." I tug open the last cupboard, my mouth pulling to the side when I find nothing larger than a dinner plate, which won't do. "There has been so much going on lately; it will be nice to relax a little and enjoy the holidays. I'm looking forward to a peaceful, calm season. I am not working at the diner anymore, so I don't have the stress of working two jobs. The Bravery Bakery is going well, thanks to my beautiful baking assistant."

Marianne takes a bow. She's making light of the praise she is due, but I mean it sincerely. Without her coming over after her shifts at the library a couple times a week, I would never have been able to open the bakery, and I certainly wouldn't be where I am today. Expanding my business to include catering parties wasn't in the business plan, but when I told Marianne about Nick and Nancy's request, she pushed me to accept the job, telling me it was too early in the game to start limiting my business.

She was right, as usual.

I tuck a stray blonde curl back into my bun, frowning at my best friend. "I'm not sure what to put the cupcakes on," I admit to Marianne as Nick strolls into the kitchen. "Hi, Nick. Lovely house you have here. And the decorations are spectacular. How long did all of this take you?"

Nick is dressed as an off-duty Santa Claus. He is clad in dress pants with a red suit jacket over his crisp white collared shirt covering his bulbous belly. His white beard is neatly trimmed in an arc two inches from his chin. His snow-colored hair is combed neatly, curling at his neck. He's even got that jolly twinkle in his eye that makes you want to promise you've been very good this year, so he brings you a new doll.

He opens the oven and peeks at the ham. "Oh, we start decorating around Halloween. It takes a fair bit of time to get it all just right. And we keep adding to the collection every year, so it gets a little more lavish each time. Did you see the array of nutcrackers? I started collecting them when I came home from the war, and never stopped. I'd like to say I only buy one a year, but that would make me easily two hundred years old." He chortles and closes the oven door. "Thanks for taking over the desserts this year, girls. I can actually greet my guests, and Nancy wasn't up all night baking. Quite the luxury."

"It's no trouble." I pop open one of the cupcake boxes. "You don't happen to have a tray, do you? Something we can set our cupcakes on."

Nick motions to the pantry. "Top shelf." The doorbell rings again, bringing a laugh from the man. "A host's duty is never done. The party doesn't start until five o'clock, but our first guest arrived well before that." He checks his watch. "I guess the party has officially started now. A bunch of people just got here."

Marianne shakes her head with a smile. "Who was the first guest?"

Nick bats his hand to excuse his mild complaining. "Delia. She likes to look at all the nutcrackers, see if she can spot the new ones."

Delia is known to be the town gossip, but I didn't realize she was so fascinated with nutcrackers. I personally think the things are a tad creepy, but to each their own, I guess. Though, I can see the appeal of coming early to scope out the massive amounts of decorations. It takes time to absorb it all.

I make my way around the kitchen and throw open the pantry door, hoping to find the perfect tray (or at this point, any clean tray).

I shriek when a person tumbles out at me. Someone must have been propped up against the closed door on the inside of the pantry, because the second I open it, the man falls onto me, knocking me over and pinning me to the tile. The back of my head slams on the floor, causing the room to spin.

Marianne bleats her distress as she darts over to us. "Oh! Charlotte, are you okay?"

Something is jabbing me in the chest while I flail after having the wind knocked out of me. I have no idea how to make heads or tails of the heavy body until Marianne helps me roll the man off me, splaying him on the floor to my left. Marianne helps me up, brushing me off while I shudder, confused and thoroughly frightened that someone fell asleep inside the pantry, standing up.

Only when I gather my wits about me and cast down to examine the person, the knife sticking out of his chest throws my theory of narcolepsy out the window. I rub my sternum, realizing now that the thing poking me was the handle of a kitchen knife.

Marianne shrieks while I pale. I drop to my knees beside the man, noting that the blood on his shirt is partially dried, while some of the crimson is sticking to my shirt.

I am wearing a dead man's blood.

Marianne covers her mouth with her hand, stuffing in a cry of anguish. It is clear that this man is not going to be getting up ever again.

My scream slices through the merriment of the Christmas music, bringing several people to the kitchen.

Worried cries splinter out through the home when the scene unfolds to the partygoers. "What did you do?" someone asks in horror. "Is that Tom? Oh, no!"

It is then I realize that I am kneeling beside a dead body, looking very much like the killer smack in the middle of Santa Claus' kitchen.

I am never delivering cupcakes again.

GUILTY

*I*f I have blinked twice in the past five minutes, that would be a surprise. Shock is still roiling through my system. My body is screaming that it is in need of a shower. I had a dead man fall on top of me. This calls for the industrial strength cleanser. Maybe a decontaminant shower.

Maybe a vacation.

Sheriff Flowers must be saving my interview for last. I am not allowed to leave while he is taking his time interviewing everyone else at the party. Though, to call this a party now is a far cry from what it has become—a somber affair with decadent food. Still, I am expected to sit amid the sliced ham and side dishes and wait for the sheriff to get to me.

"Honey, eat some food. You look pale." Nancy hands me a plate.

I have forgotten the functionality of my hands, so the plate remains in the air between us. "I'm not hungry right now but thank you."

"A fifteen-pound ham, and hardly anyone has eaten a thing." Nancy sets the plate down and shakes her head. "I'm sorry. I perpetually feed people when I'm nervous. Ignore me."

Marianne hasn't left my side, nor has her hand left mine since she helped me to my feet and then led me to sit down at a chair in the dining room. With her free hand, she pockets her phone. "Agnes just texted me. She, Karen and Winifred were on their tour of nude ice sculptures, but they're trying to find a bus back to Sweetwater Falls. I'm sure they'll be here before long."

I turn my chin toward Marianne, my body still tensed. "Tell them not to rush back. They've been talking about this tour for weeks. They booked a hotel and everything so they could make a vacation out of it. There's nothing they can do now. It's not like they can bring Tom back to life."

Marianne casts me a wary look, but texts Agnes to stay put.

I can hear Delia talking at top volume from the next room, her words clear enough between her intermittent sobs. "Tom was my neighbor. I can't believe someone would kill him and shove him inside a pantry! Who would do such a thing?"

Who, indeed. I can see the sheriff has a few theories,

pulling couples aside to ask them when they arrived at the party, and if they noticed anything off when they got here. My stomach is in knots because I know he is saving me for last. Even though I didn't murder Tom, I am still sweating like a criminal under a spotlight.

I didn't know him because I didn't make the time to know him. I know he made stew at the Halloween Festival, but I can recall the details of the stew better than our brief interactions.

Now I'll never get to truly know him.

The Christmas music has a macabre feel to it, now that the evening is painted with murder. But when I hear a voice that always makes me turn my head, the room becomes a little less dim. Relief spreads over me when Logan Flowers comes into view, bringing the last vestiges of the sunshine with him.

He doesn't wait for an explanation but helps me up from my chair so he can squish me in his arms. "I came as soon as I got the call."

It's clear he was off-duty tonight, since he is wearing a hunter green polo that sets off the grassy hue of his eyes perfectly. But not even the most beautiful man in the world can erase the clammy sensation curdling my stomach.

Marianne stands beside me, her hand on my back. "It's Tom, Logan. Tom was dead and shoved standing up in the pantry just over there. When Charlotte opened up the pantry to see if there were any trays to put the cupcakes on, he fell straight onto her, tackling her to the ground." Marianne grimaces. "Well, not so much tackling, since I'm pretty sure you have to be alive to tackle somebody. But you know what I mean."

Logan hisses his disapproval. "Are you hurt? Did you hit your head on the floor?"

The back of my head is a little sore, but as a man is dead, complaining about a booboo hardly seems appropriate. "I really just want to get out of here, but I don't think I'm allowed to leave until your dad has questioned me. He told me not to go anywhere."

Logan's nostrils flare. "I'll handle it. Marianne, are you okay?"

Marianne's head bobs. "Anxious to get out of here, but otherwise fine. Tom didn't land on me."

Logan sits me back down on my chair in the dining room as if I am fragile and in need of tender care, which I guess isn't too far off the mark at the moment. He stalks into the living room, where I hear the murmur of the sheriff interacting with his agitated son.

"Put it back," a man says, his voice coming from the kitchen. I can hear the person talking from my spot in the dining room, but I can't see him. About half the guests have been released and sent home after they gave their statements to the sheriff. I'm not sure who all is here at the moment.

Delia's voice is hard to miss. Even though I am sitting in the dining room and she is in the kitchen, I can picture her frizzy ponytail plain as day. "It's nothing. Honestly. Nick has hundreds of these things. Look around this place. No one should have this many. He won't miss it."

"Don't you think they've been through enough tonight?" the person scolds Delia.

But Delia scoffs in response. "You're kidding me, right? There was a body stuffed in their pantry. Nick and Nancy killed Tom. Isn't it obvious?"

"You don't know that. There are so many people coming in and out of here. It could have been anyone."

"Right. Did you see any guests come in the front door with a full-grown human in their purse? And Tom wasn't invited to this party. I know that for a fact. Tom didn't come to the party and die during the appetizers at the hand of one of the guests. He wasn't supposed to be here."

The man's voice lowers. "Well, the caterers came in through the side door. They could have sneaked Tom's body inside and shoved it in the pantry, then pretended to discover it." There is a pause for Delia's gasp. "I'll bet that's exactly what happened."

If I was pale before, I must be positively ashen now.

Delia scoffs at him. "Charlotte McKay? The new girl? I don't think so. And Marianne wouldn't hurt a fly. She's a pixie. They were just at the wrong place at the wrong time."

The tightness in my chest loosens a little when Delia defends us. That's good. She's the town gossip, so whatever she thinks is spread far and wide. Not that her opinion constitutes as evidence, but still, best not give the town any ammunition to fuel an already damning situation.

Marianne squeezes my hand. "We obviously didn't kill Tom. The evidence will prove that."

"How?" I wonder aloud, grateful it wasn't just me who overheard the upsetting exchange. "All the evidence points toward us!"

Marianne shakes her head. "Then we're not looking close enough. The body was here well before five o'clock, right? Because we arrived at a quarter till. Nick and Nancy had already cleaned up from cooking before we got here, so there's not a huge window of time the killer could have stashed the body in here."

Delia's voice carries, interrupting our pondering. "Sure, but that doesn't mean anything."

"Charlotte is dating the sheriff's son," the man informs her. "A cop. If anyone could get away with murder in plain sight, it would be the girl dating the guy who can hide the evidence."

Delia's conviction that we are innocent begins to waffle. "I don't know."

I cover my mouth with my hand. Sure, Logan and I are officially dating after a long stint of double dates and him coming over to hang out with Marianne and me at home. But to think people could reduce our very new relationship to a matter of devious convenience makes me sick to my stomach. "I really want to go home," I whisper to Marianne.

My best friend stands, determination tightening her dainty features. "I've heard enough. That is utter nonsense." She looks six feet tall (though she is nowhere near that height) as she stomps into the kitchen. "Is there a problem? Do you two have a theory you'd like to share? Because the sheriff is right in the living room. No better time than the present to confront two coldblooded killers for a crime we reported to the police."

I tuck my sweaty hands between my knees, wanting this whole thing to be over so I don't have to endure Tom's blood on my clothes any longer. There are only a few stains, but it feels disrespectful to wear them. I didn't know Tom all that well.

And now I never will.

Marianne comes back to me clearly disgruntled. "I cannot believe some people. We're leaving. I don't want to listen to another word of that garbage. Come on, Charlotte. I'll drive you home."

"I can't," I remind her. "The sheriff told me to sit down."

Logan rounds the corner with his father, who appears tired and mildly agitated with himself. The sheriff has the same dimpled chin as Logan, but the shared charm stops there. "Charlotte, I'm sorry. I wanted you to sit down because you'd just taken a spill."

I blink up at the sheriff, confused. "You don't need to question me?"

The sheriff's shoulders lower. "The stab wound suggests he was killed hours ago, if not yesterday. You were with Logan most of the day, so no, you're in the clear." He motions to my sallow complexion. "Plus, I'm not sure you can fake that sort of shock. You're free to go home."

Gratitude lifts my spirits just enough for my body to allow Logan to pull me up from my chair. "I have to stay here and help out," Logan says to me.

"You mean you have to do your job?" I try to smile at him, but it comes out all wrong. "The nerve."

Logan's smile also appears forced. "You joke, but I feel terrible sending you home while I stay here. As soon as I can clock out, I'll head over to your place to check on you, okay?"

Marianne stands beside me. "I'll stay with her, Logan. Take your time."

"My purse," I tell Marianne. "It should be in the kitchen."

"On it!" But Marianne comes back a minute later with empty hands. "Are you sure it's in the kitchen?"

I really want to go home, but that sort of task is impossible without car keys.

Logan casts around. "I'll check the living room."

Marianne points to the wall. "I'll search the dining room."

I lean against the wall, taking in the milling guests.

Most are murmuring in clusters around the giant living room. The decorations that just an hour ago seemed sparkly and beautiful now look dim and ominous.

When a patron I've seen a few times at the diner passes by, I grab her sleeve. "Excuse me, have you seen my purse? It's brown. Not too big. I left it in the kitchen, but I can't seem to find it."

The woman points to a smaller room with glass doors to the side of the entryway. "The coats and purses and whatnot were put in there. Maybe someone added yours to the pile."

I meander on wobbly legs past the giant Christmas tree in the hallway toward the study, noting the pretty leather chair and marbled wallpaper upon entering. Nick and Nancy really don't leave any detail out when they have a design aesthetic in mind. Everything looks expertly chosen for the room. I search through the purses and coats, but still don't see mine anywhere.

"You should tell the sheriff," I hear Nick say in a hushed voice just outside the glass door.

"And bring more scandal to our house? It's not relevant," Nancy replies. "As far as the two of us are concerned, the only people in this house were our invited guests. Helen was never here."

My spine stiffens. I stop moving so I can make out their exchange.

Helen is the chef at the Spaghetti Scarf. She has a passion for pure cooking and homemade garlic bread.

Anyone who loves delicious food usually becomes a fast friend, which is what we became when we first met earlier this year.

Nick's voice is gruff now. "But Helen was in here. She made the ham. She delivered it and came in through the side door. I didn't make sure she was only bringing in the food and not also a body! Did you?"

The fretting in Nancy's tone leads me to believe that she had nothing to do with the murder. She is just as much a victim of happenstance as I am in this whole mess. "No, but it's Helen. She wouldn't murder anyone."

"Well, someone did, and we let them into our house!"

"Nick, don't you dare tell the sheriff that someone else made my famous Christmas ham. Our guests talk about it all year. If they found out that I never made it, but hire Helen every year, I'll be ruined!"

Nick's scolding isn't lost on me. "Would you like to go to jail over ham? Because that's what might happen, Nancy. The sheriff needs someone to focus his search on, other than us. Helen was in here, unsupervised."

Nancy pinches the bridge of her nose. "Oh, this is so awful!"

I wait until the two shuffle away before emerging from the study, my nerves sufficiently shattered.

I cannot imagine the person with whom Helen would be angry enough to kill. And why Tom? Did he have any enemies? Who would murder him and frame Nick and

Nancy for the crime? Do the three of them have a connection of which I am unaware?

The finger is about to be pointed at Helen. If I am going to save my friend from being accused of murder, I am going to have to get to the bottom of who killed Tom myself.

3

TOMATOES AND TEA

*M*arianne slept over last night. She has been by my side ever since I discovered Tom's body. "Are you sure you don't want me to stay home?" she asks.

"What would the library do without their head librarian?" I reply with a bump of my hip to hers. "Go on. I'm alright. That hot shower when we got home last night did me a world of good." When she hesitates, I shoo her towards the front door. "I'm fine, I promise."

After Marianne leaves, I set to making my schedule for the week. Now that the catering job is behind me— more or less—I can wrap my mind around the rest of the orders coming in. Cupcakes are available for pickup twice a week. I like that setup because it ensures I'm not baking every single day of my life. Today is my shopping day, so I take inventory and write down all the ingredients I will need to fill the orders coming in through my website.

I never thought I would be able to say those sorts of sentences and apply them to my business. I always dreamed of owning a cupcake bakery, but I never actually thought my dream would come true. Gratitude fills me as I jot down ingredients, grateful that most everything I need is fairly inexpensive and easily accessible.

My positive flow is interrupted often because about every other minute, I freeze when the image of Tom's body falling on top of me from the pantry slams into my brain, unbidden. But I'm getting better at pushing aside the visual so I can do things like breathe.

The stab wound on Tom's chest was surrounded by mostly dried blood. The few bits of crimson that stuck to my clothing came in dots and small patches, not wet splatters that suggest he was killed ten minutes before we got there.

I turn to my goldfish, who is swimming in her bowl, flicking her tail atop the counter in the cheery yellow kitchen. "The blood was mostly dried, but not all the way," I say to Buttercream while she flips her tiny fin at me. "The sheriff was right. Tom probably died yesterday, but not right before we got there. The murder could have happened at Nick and Nancy's, but that place was so clean, I'm sure a blood splatter would have been visible."

Unless it was too clean, my mind replies, playing devil's advocate.

I speak aloud to my fish. Buttercream swims from side to side, watching me as if she understands everything I am saying. "No, no. Tom's murder most likely happened outside the house. His body was brought in while they were doing other things, too distracted to notice."

I can almost hear my fish ask me, "How do you not notice a man being dragged into a house?"

"Good question. I mean, it's a big house. It's not unthinkable that they were in a different part of the house, especially if the person in question was sneaking in." I pause, my mouth pulling to the side. "Which would mean they might have their own key."

Now that I'm thinking about Nick and Nancy, I remember I need to cash their check. I brew myself some tea and put it in a travel mug, so I have some serenity at hand in case the memory of the party gone wrong last night becomes too difficult to shake.

I brew a second cup because I cannot let another day pass before I talk to Helen. She should know what accusations might be coming for her. I remember her schedule pretty well from when I used to bake cupcakes to sell at the Spaghetti Scarf where Helen is the chef. If I time it right, I will get there right around her first break of the day.

I miss Winifred. She, Karen and Agnes have been away for a handful of days, living it up on their vacation. I'm glad Marianne talked them out of coming home early. They deserve a little escape.

I snatch up my brown purse and drive to the Spaghetti

Scarf, inhaling the garlic-laden air with a smile on my face. My mouth waters, even though normally the prospect of garlic bread and pasta at ten in the morning is truly gag-worthy. Notes of garlic, shallots and tomato sauce hit my senses. The tomato is so strong that I scarcely remember any other smell exists.

The hostess lets me in, even though they're not open for business yet, recognizing me from when I did business with them. I sneak into the long and narrow kitchen, smiling at Helen as I watch her chop with equal amounts of gusto and precision. I love that I have friends who take pride in their work—especially when their work happens to be food.

Helen is in her fifties, her dark hair matted to her fore-head by the hairnet. Her round face is red and sweaty, her small pink nose crinkling when she smells the next onion, then tosses it in the trash because it doesn't pass muster.

I wait for her to put the knife down before I make my presence known, so I don't spook her. "Hi, Helen. I stopped by to bring you some tea and a cupcake."

Helen straightens, turning to me as worry melts to a congenial smile. "Hi, Charlotte. Were you standing there long? Sorry, my mind was somewhere else."

I tilt my head to the side. "Somewhere happy or some-where sad?" It's a simplistic question, but judging by her weighted shoulders, I know it's a valid query. I set my things down and grab a knife off the magnetic strip on the black backsplash. I start chopping green bell peppers so

Helen can take a load off and actually enjoy a sip of the tea I brought her.

"It's ten in the morning, and already it's been a long day," Helen admits, swiping at her dark hair beneath the hairnet. "Thanks, honey. This tea is good, and you know I love your cupcakes."

"What's going on?"

Helen shoots me a knowing look. "I think you can guess a little bit about my headache if you've stopped by at random to cheer me up." She lowers her chin. "Sheriff Flowers came to my house this morning to ask me if I had anything to do with Tom's death."

I grimace that my guess was right on the mark. "Oh, Helen. I was afraid that might have happened. Tell me all about it. Sit down while I do the lunch prep."

She takes me up on my offer, sighing dejectedly. She takes a long drink before spilling her secrets. "I guess the agreement that I keep quiet about Nick and Nancy's party feast is off, now that my name was brought into the mix. They are the only two who could have told the sheriff that I was in their home. It's the right thing to do, but still, it feels like they're trying to point the finger at me."

I keep my eyes on the peppers and carrots while I chop. "I'm not following."

Helen leans back, inhaling the fragrance of the tea. "It's a secret, what I do for them. Their Christmas party gets bigger every year, and Nick and Nancy aren't getting any younger. I don't know why they don't just tell people they don't make the Christmas dinner. It's not like anyone will look down on them. Pride is weird."

"Nancy doesn't cook the Christmas dinner?" I overheard Nancy saying as much to Nick.

"I've been cooking her Christmas dinner for years now. She pays me well enough, so I like doing it. Last year, though, there were some issues with her payment." She lowers her voice and leans in, even though we are the only two in the kitchen. "Her check bounced. When I told her about it, she hemmed and hawed and took a month to pay me. I told her this year that the money had to be up front. She got all bent out of shape, but the only other option was to cook it herself, which she isn't willing to do. She was mad at me for charging what I'm worth and not coming down on my price." Helen shakes her head, her jaw firm. "I don't do that. I have a job, so I don't need the extra work at the expense of my sanity. I like Nancy, but I told her this would be the last year I do it. Haggling with anyone in Sweetwater Falls isn't how I like to spend my time."

I grimace at the notion of having to haggle with Mrs. Claus. "I can imagine. So you made all the food, and what? You dropped it off earlier in the day?"

Helen nods. "Around four o'clock yesterday. I know some of her guests like to get there early to look at all their decorations. I saw a few in the driveway, but I brought the food around through the side entrance, so Nancy could keep up the charade that she cooks a huge feast every year."

"That's nice of you. The ham smelled incredible." I offer her a small smile. "I delivered the cupcakes."

"Did you get paid up front?"

"Half up front, half upon delivery. She gave me a check for the other half." Though, now I have a niggling worry that the check might not go through, if my experience is anything like Helen's was last year.

"I'm sure the check will cash," Helen says as though she can read my mind. "Makes me happy to see you following your dreams, opening up a cupcake bakery out of your home." She picks up the cupcake. "This is quality baking, young lady."

"Thanks." I need all the information about the party. There are too many pieces of the puzzle missing. "When you dropped off your food, did you happen to go into the pantry?"

Helen's mouth pulls to the side. "No need. I take all my garbage with me so Nancy and Nick don't have to haul it to the curb. I bring everything already made and they have the chafing dishes set out and ready for me. After doing it for them this many years, I've got a pretty flawless system."

That means Tom's body could have been there even before four o'clock. I'm not narrowing down my search at all.

At least I'm giving Helen a bit of a break on an already rough morning.

"Did you notice anything out of place? Anything odd?"

Helen shrugs. "The kitchen was a mess. I'm not sure

that's odd, but it certainly was unexpected. I mean, she didn't have to do any sort of cooking, but there were tons of dishes in the sink and the counters needed a good wipe down."

My mouth pulls to the side. "When I got there, the kitchen was immaculate. I remember thinking how impressive that was, being that I thought she had also cooked a feast in that kitchen for fifty people. It makes more sense that it was clean when I factor in you doing the cooking that day. But why would it be dirty? Did you clean it up? Because I've got to say, you did a fantastic job."

Helen shakes her head. "I wiped down the counters, but nothing else. I was hired to make and deliver dinner, not do dishes."

I admire the ability to respect oneself enough not to be a pushover.

"Huh. I guess she did a deep clean after you left."

Helen chuckles at my guess. "That would be surprising. Nancy doesn't like to get her hands dirty." She takes another drink of her tea. "Could have been the housekeeper. I know Nancy has one."

I nod, wondering how many people were in and out of that house that the sheriff now has to keep track of. I wonder if he has any time to sit down, now that all this drama has been brought to the precious small town of Sweetwater Falls.

I finish the lunch prep while Helen and I exchange banter on lighter topics. I like listening to Helen talk about working under the new management, and how her new boss honors the integrity of the ingredients, and the original recipes that made the Spaghetti Scarf a restaurant worth coming to. Talking food with a friend is one of the best ways to spend a morning.

If not for Tom's murder, our visit would be completely perfect.

When I leave the Spaghetti Scarf, I have a deeper friendship with Helen, but I am no closer to solving Tom's murder.

4

ONE DOLLAR BILL

One of my favorite things to do is pass by the Nosy Newsy—the newsstand in town run by Frank. It's not because I necessarily need to purchase a magazine or newspaper, and it's certainly not because I need any of the candy bars he sells. No, there is an oblong box of purple and white flowers at the stand where a certain someone and I exchange love notes.

I stroll to the stand, sharing a head bob with Frank as I beeline to the flowers, searching beneath the petals for the note that has my name on it. No matter what sort of day I am having, a smile always finds me if Logan has left me a sweet little note.

I take out my letter and hide my message for Logan behind the stems, picturing his smile when he fishes out his note.

My goodness, Logan is handsome. Even in my imagination, his features are flawless.

"How are the lovebirds doing today?" Frank asks, running his fingers through his greasy black hair. "Anything new?"

"Other than Tom's death? No, nothing new. How's Delia holding up?"

It's supposed to be some big secret that Frank has a crush on Delia, so I make sure no one is within earshot when I ask him about her.

The tips of Frank's ears turn pink at the mention of her name. "She's upset." He ducks his head and glances around to make sure his words stay between us. "I brought her coffee this morning so she could vent about the party."

I try not to tease him too badly over such blatant cuteness. "That was thoughtful of you, Frank."

He straightens a magazine on the rack. "Shame about Tom."

"Did you know him well?"

"Not as well as Delia. They were neighbors. Though not exactly the friendly kind. Tom had one of those yippy dogs that used to wake her up every morning. She's pretty shaken up, having seen the body and all. First time she's ever seen a dead body. That'll turn anyone's dreams into nightmares."

"Sure." Sadness pings at my soul. "Did Tom have any family? I didn't know him. Only saw him in passing at town events."

"No kids. Never married. His dog was his closest friend, I'm guessing, though he wasn't exactly without those. Nobody hated him. I can't imagine he's done all that many controversial things in his life. Poor guy. He lived for the town festivals. The Christmas Festival won't be the same without him."

"Was he a big part of it?"

"He got real competitive," Frank chuckles. "Always wanted to win best lemonade at the Lemon Festival. Bragged to anyone who would listen about the quality of his Halloween stew. I love the people who go all out for the town events. Makes me want to be more involved. I like seeing people get excited about stuff. It's contagious."

"Absolutely."

Frank dips his head in my direction. "Delia told me Tom's dead body fell on you and crushed you. Told me you got a concussion from being slammed to the ground when you opened the pantry door. You alright?"

My hip cocks to the side. "I didn't have a concussion. But the other stuff is spot on. It was upsetting, to say that least. But I'm alright. Just trying to figure out how Tom's body could have made its way into the kitchen with a house full of people and no one noticed a thing. It's odd, right?"

Frank arches a dark brow at me. "You really think that's what happened?"

My mouth pulls to the side. "I can't imagine any other explanation."

"You can't imagine that Nick and Nancy didn't want revenge on Tom? You can't imagine that a husband and wife would do anything for each other, even over the smallest thing?"

"I have no idea what you're talking about. Did Nick and Nancy not get along with Tom?"

"Tom wasn't invited to the party. Every year, people hope for an invitation to Nick and Nancy's big party, but they accused Tom of stealing one of their nutcrackers last year, so Tom wasn't invited back. It was a big fight over at Bill's Diner the day after their Christmas party last year. Tom swears he didn't take it, and Nick and Nancy swear he did."

"Do you really think that Nick and Nancy would murder a man over a toy? They have hundreds of those nutcrackers all over their house. How would they notice one is missing?"

Frank stands with his feet further than shoulder-width apart, his arms crossed over his chest. "I think people get crazy around the holidays. It's not outside the realm of possibility that a fight turned into a feud. Just last month, I saw Tom walking down the street. Nick and Nancy saw him coming and they crossed to the other side, so they didn't have to go near each other."

"That's sad. I mean really, really sad. It's a nutcracker."

"To you and me it's just a nutcracker, but to Nick and Nancy? You never know what random items mean to a person." Frank motions for me to come beside the cash register with him. Hidden from public view but still in plain sight on the side of his register is a dollar bill secured to the steel with transparent packing tape. "See that? To anyone with eyes, it's a normal dollar bill. But to me, this dollar is worth tens of thousands."

"How's that?"

Frank's finger traces across the bill. "This was my first ever dollar I made at this newsstand. My father was my very first customer. Made it a point to get here an hour before I officially opened on my first day, so he could be the first person to support me." Sadness dots Frank's memory. "He died a year after that. This dollar is worth a lot to me because it's a symbol of my father's faith in me. He didn't just love me with words, but with actions that meant something to the both of us."

I reach over and hold onto Frank's hand because after a heartfelt story like that, I can't not. "Your father sounds like a good man."

"The very best." Frank squeezes my hand once. "My point is that you never know how special a thing might be to someone. Maybe that particular nutcracker Tom is supposed to have stolen was special in some way to Nick and Nancy. Maybe Tom didn't just steal a toy, but made off with a precious memory. If everything in my register was stolen, I'd be upset, but I would get over it. But if a person came along and stole my father's dollar?" He shakes his head. "I'm not sure I would get out of bed the next day."

When Delia's voice slices through the tender moment,

I perk up. "Well, what a surprise seeing you here, Charlotte. I didn't think you'd be out and about the day after having a dead body fall on you."

Though people have not stopped mentioning the horror of how Tom's body was discovered, the way Delia phrases it cuts through my ribs, leaving me with a ghastly flinch. "Hi, Delia." I drop Frank's hand and tuck Logan's note into my pocket. "You doing okay? Last night was rough on everyone."

Delia looks put together and peppy, her makeup done and her chestnut hair up in a frizzy topknot. "I'm dealing with it all. How's Logan?"

I tilt my head to the side. "He's okay, last I checked. But I'm sure he had a long night after everything that happened. I can't imagine any of the officers are feeling happy today."

"But you two are still together, right?" She motions between Frank and me. "Because I saw the two of you holding hands and was floored. I really didn't see that coming."

Frank's eyes go wide. "What? No. I was telling her a story, is all."

Delia grins at me, though there is a maniacal quality to the showing of her teeth. "I can't remember the last time I held a man's hand whom I wasn't dating all so I could listen to a story."

Horror washes through me. "Delia, what are you saying? Frank, I'm sorry. Did I make you uncomfortable?"

"No, I mean, obviously not. Delia, you're reading too much into it. Charlotte's a child."

I narrow my eyes at him, wanting to argue that I can't possibly be vastly younger than he is. But that hardly helps my case of making sure Delia knows I am not flirting with Frank, of all people.

Frank has a crush on Delia, and she knows full well of his feelings. Apparently, they are at the awkward phase of feeling out whether or not the other is romantically involved with someone else, so they can decide if a relationship is worth the gamble.

And I am caught smack in the middle.

Oh, joy.

I hold up my hands. "I'll be going. Have a nice morning, Delia. Good to see you. Lovely, as usual." I don't bother waving goodbye to Frank, for fear that a simple gesture might be misinterpreted.

5

SWEETWATER FOUNTAINS

My cheeks are red as I stroll through the main thoroughfare of Sweetwater Falls. I take my time acquainting myself with the city, since I don't have any pressing orders to fill today. In my purse, I have a stack of flyers that I pass out to each business I stop at. I shake hands and get to know the people in the small town I love, letting them know that my cupcakery is open for business, and now caters parties, should they have any special events in their stores.

I never used to be a girl who fought for what I wanted, but even though business is booming, I am not used to having a day off with nothing to do. Every person I can add to my list of clients is a boon to my business. Word of mouth is my bread and butter, so I waste no time in spreading the word that I am open and ready to fill Sweetwater Falls with sugar and frosting.

The Thanksgiving decorations came down last week, leaving space for the people on ladders to hang lavish wreaths and wrap the lampposts with garland and red Christmas lights. I love that there is a plan to celebrate everything here. I adore the enthusiasm with which each holiday is treated. It's all I can do to keep up with the meticulous planning and make sure my business is ready to match the cheer that is being put up all around me.

Rip embraces his role as the town selectman, conducting his minions toward the clipboard in his hands. "Last year we used three strands of lights per lamppost. I don't want us skimping this year. Either just as good as last year or better, people. Make sure each strand is working perfectly before you start wrapping it around, otherwise it's a headache to get it unwrapped and replaced. Each light counts, people!"

I should be thinking of a Christmas flavor to add to my website. My Halloween cupcake of the month went over like gangbusters. I want something equally spectacular for December.

The first thing to come to mind is candy cane, because that is the staple candy of the season. But I worry it's been overdone, so I keep thinking. I have a handful of flavors on my website every month, plus a new flavor of the month that is available only for a limited time. Being that it's December now, I need to get on the ball and really step up my game.

When I let myself into a store I have never visited

called Sweetwater Fountains, I wonder why I never took the time to come here before. It is nestled between a candle shop and a pet store, both of which have storefronts that look cute and well maintained. I guess I assumed that a store called Sweetwater Fountains would have industrial fountains for schools and parks and whatnot. But when I walk in, I am pleasantly surprised to see a smattering of tabletop Zen fountains meant to instill peace in the purchaser.

A smile comes over me as I inhale the fragrance of evergreen. It smells like Christmas in here, and I love it. The tinkling of several water fountains going at once takes my worry over the misunderstanding with Frank and Delia and ushers it to the side. Now the forefront of my mind is open to the happiness that comes with pure peace. I didn't realize how simple it would be to relax when the sound of water falling is the backdrop to your thoughts, but I am really loving this store.

A woman seems to float toward me, her skirt—or skirts —flowing out with each step. She looks straight out of the seventies, complete with a peace sign on a rope around her neck. She wears several crystals embedded in the jewelry around her wrists. Her smile is unaffected by the world at large, her red hair billowing out to her waist as she greets me. "Hello. Welcome to Sweetwater Fountains. I'm Jeannette. How are you on this fine morning?"

I am sure I had concerns before I walked into her establishment, but I cannot recall them now. "You know, I think I'm good." I glance around the shop, taking in various windchimes with waterfall designs and stones meant for healing and whatnot. There are mirrored balls that look like lawn ornaments, perched in birdbaths with water cascading over them. "Your store is lovely. I can't believe I've never been in here before."

Jeanette smells like pachouli and flowers. "Well, let me show you around. Over here, we have fountains of all sizes. Indoor and outdoor, tabletop and wall high. Some come with Tibetan singing bowl music when they are running to help cleanse your negative energy."

I never give much thought to energies, but after having a dead man fall on me, I'm not about to sneeze at anything that might bring a little serenity into my life. "I don't have anything like that. They're all so pretty."

"Tell me about yourself. What brings you in today? I can usually match a person with their perfect fountain once they open up a bit and express what brought them to consider welcoming some additional peace into their life."

I dig out a flyer and hand it to her, my eyes glued to a fountain that might sit on a desk. It's simple and unassuming, but the small trickle of water has me transfixed. "I actually came in here to introduce myself to all the business owners of Sweetwater Falls. I just opened my own business—a cupcake bakery—and I wanted to tell you about it. But now that I'm in here, I kind of don't want to leave. It's so peaceful."

Jeanette's smile is calm and lovely. "Then I'm doing it

right. Tell me about your business." She skims over the flyer. "Oh, I've heard of you. You're the new girl. Winifred's niece. I love Winifred. She bought a bird fountain from me years ago. It was designed to bring its owner good luck and a long life."

I chuckle at the perfect wish for someone like my great-aunt. "That's about right. The Live Forever Club has enough luck to get them out of whatever mess they find themselves in. It's a beautiful bird fountain. Lives up to its name."

"I'm glad to hear that. And now you're selling cupcakes out of her house?"

"Yes. All ordering is done online. I cater parties and do individual orders."

Jeanette extends her hand to me. "How about I put a few flyers by the checkout? A little extra advertising for you."

Warmth fills my heart. The people of this town rarely disappoint, always going above and beyond in their sweetness. I am getting desperate for a kitchen to cook in, so I don't keep taking over Aunt Winnie's kitchen, but the business has to stay in Sweetwater Falls, where the options are limited. I couldn't dream of taking my business outside this precious small town.

I cast Jeanette a grateful smile. "That would be amazing. Thank you." I point to the small fountain that caught my eye. "What can you tell me about this one?" I can picture it in the library, sitting at the circulation desk and offering peace to all who pass by. Plus, it's set in a lavender bowl, which is Marianne's favorite color.

"Ah, that fountain has amethyst stones mixed in with the other rocks."

I peer inside, noting the glow of the lavender crystals that match the color of the basin. "So pretty. I mean, everything in here is nice, but that one... There's something about it."

Jeanette scoots aside the other fountains on the display so I can see the one on which I am fixated. "Amethyst is a soothing stone. It calms nerves and keeps clarity in check."

"All of those things sound amazing for a library. Could you show me how it plugs in and whatnot?"

Jeanette goes over all the details, and with each sentence, I am more and more convinced that I have found the perfect Christmas present for Marianne.

"People need clarity and calm in a library, right? I was thinking this might be a good Christmas gift for Marianne."

"Absolutely. Think of the calm you felt when you entered my store. With a fountain to greet readers, they might just stay longer and read more if they forget about the previous rush of their day."

"I like everything about this. I'll take it."

My smile is beaming when Jeanette takes the fountain down and puts it in a box for me. "Each fountain is handmade by me. One of a kind, so you know the peace and the calm was made just for you."

"Oh, I love that. Makes it special."

"You know, I've got an extra filter I can throw in for you. It's in the back. Might take me a minute, because part of my inventory is currently on top of a stove back there." She rolls her eyes at herself. "Organization isn't my strong suit."

I snicker at her self-deprecating remark and wave her off.

I like this place. When she comes in from the back, Jeanette even goes so far as to giftwrap the box in a lavender paper while I take my time perusing her various items. While they are all nice, none grabbed my attention as much as the one for Marianne.

Jeanette's voice lowers, even though we are the only two in the store. "I heard about the business with Tom's death. You might want to spend some time in here, letting the singing bowl music cleanse any negative energy. I'm guessing last night wasn't entirely restful for you."

I shake my head. "I wish I knew who could do something so terrible. Murder and then shoving the body inside a pantry on the night of a party? That takes forethought and planning."

"Indeed, it does. I can't imagine who would do such a thing." She gets out a silver bow and wraps it around the gift, making it extra special. "Tom bought a windchime from me not too long ago. It was for releasing any emotional blockages. He had a few frustrations he was working through. I hope it helped."

"Frustrations?"

"Don't we all have them? Tom complained about someone throwing chocolate candies into his yard. His dog, Beanie, could have eaten them and died, had he not found them. He bought a pet water fountain for Beanie not long after that. The fountain was for longevity." Her expression melts to melancholy. "Maybe I should have switched those two things. Tom was the one who needed longevity, and Beanie needed some emotional blockage drained. That dog was very tightly wound."

My heart goes out to her. "I'm sure the dog heard the windchimes, and they calmed him as much as they were able."

"I hope so. Such a terrible thing. I never like to think of someone passing away well before their time. Not here. Not when there is so much love in our town." She glances over at me. "Do you like it here so far?"

"Apart from someone trying to poison a dog, I like Sweetwater Falls just fine. I thought I would be here to help Winifred around the house, but she's been more of a help to me. I'm trying to wrap my mind around what to get the Live Forever Club for Christmas. They are so special to me, so I know their gifts have to be something special, too."

I expect a business owner to recommend her own goods to sell me, but Jeanette replies with a serene, "The right gift will come to you when you are ready to receive it."

I like everything about Jeanette, especially when she

takes a bracelet off her wrist and loops it around mine. "Here. This is for serenity. After the ordeal you suffered through yesterday, I think you need this more than I do."

I gape at her generosity. A fresh wave of gooey affection stirs in my chest. Even though yesterday was filled with horror, today I am reminded that there is nothing so terrible that a little kindness cannot cure.

6

BAKING AND GUESSING

*M*arianne takes hold of the mixing bowl, eyeing the batter because it is lumpier than it should be. "I don't like the look of this batch. Are you sure we did it right?"

I love having a friend to pal around with while I work. Though I am nowhere near as busy as I was when I was working two jobs, part of the reason I like having a friend to bake with has little to do with the workload and much to do with the conversation and companionship. "The butter wasn't as room temperature as it usually is. It'll need an extra minute in the mixer. Keep it at a low speed, otherwise the cupcakes might be too chewy and not light enough."

"I love the science part of this, even though I understand precious little of it." Marianne turns the mixer on low speed, watching the batter as if she needs to study it for an exam. "I'm impressed that you went door to door advertising your business. That's so smart. You know what Winifred would say, right?"

I smirk at her. "She would call me Charlotte the Brave."

"Yes, she would. You know I'll be taking a stack of flyers to put out at the library, right?"

"Have I ever told you that you're amazing?"

"Only once or twice. Never stop, or I'll forget and become simply pretty good."

I line the cupcake pans with festive Christmas wrappers. "I know I'm usually not all that outgoing with these sorts of things, but I kept thinking about how much faith you all had in me and how hard you worked to help me get my business off the ground. It seems disrespectful to all your effort not to push this as hard as I can, so it has a decent chance at succeeding. Bravery was a necessity."

"You're doing it, Charlotte. I mean, you're really doing it. We're up fifteen percent from last week's orders, which is up three percent from the week before. If this keeps going, you're going to have to hire help. I mean, we can keep up for now, but in another month, who knows?"

I freeze as her words sink in. "I can't even wrap my mind around that. Hiring someone? Hiring someone because we can't keep up? It's a good problem to have, but I can't imagine we'll get there anytime soon."

Marianne shrugs. "I'm just saying, your bravery is paving the way for big time success. I'm just glad to be along for the ride."

I finish lining the pans and take a moment to turn my cactus on the windowsill so a different portion of the plant will see the sun tomorrow. I've kept this thing alive for two months now, which is a feat I never thought I would be able to brag about.

As I glance out the window, my eyes fall on the bird bath in the backyard. "I went to Sweetwater Fountains," I tell Marianne once the mixer turns off. "I talked with Jeanette, who told me that someone tried to feed Beanie chocolate not too long ago. Left chocolate candies in Tom's backyard for the dog to find."

Marianne's eyes widen. "Are you serious? That's terrible!" She shakes her head. "Some people. Who would want to hurt a dog? Even a dog as annoying and yippie as Beanie. He doesn't deserve that."

My mouth pulls to the side. "Delia doesn't like Beanie," I tell her quietly. "She lives next door, and apparently there was some tension about Beanie barking early in the morning."

Marianne grimaces. "You don't think Delia would try to poison Beanie, though, would she?"

I shake my head, though I am not entirely convinced. "I don't think so. I like Delia just fine. I can't imagine she would try to murder a dog." I take the mixing bowl and start doling out portions into each liner, being careful not to get any drips on the pan. "I thought the feeling was mutual, but I'm starting to think I'm on Delia's naughty list."

"How did you manage to get on anyone's naughty list?" Marianne casts me a look of sheer disbelief.

"I stopped by the Nosy Newsy to leave Logan a note, and Frank started talking about his dad. It was a sad story, so I squeezed his hand because the situation warranted some kind of sympathy. Delia came up, and I guess it looked like we were holding hands in the romantic way. I think she got the wrong idea about why I was at Frank's stand in the first place."

Marianne snickers. "Oh, man. That's some bad timing. Doesn't she know that you're with Logan?"

I nod. "Maybe Delia thinks those kinds of boundaries don't matter to a big city tramp like me." My harsh words hit the air without filter, giving a voice to my hurt feelings. "I didn't mean anything by it."

Marianne bats away my culpability. "You don't need to waste another second of worry on that. If Delia wants to lock down Frank, then she should actually date him. You did nothing wrong. You offered friendship, which is nothing scandalous." She shakes her head as she rinses off the whisk in the sink. "Delia's just making a fuss out of nothing. It's her way."

I inhale deeply, letting Marianne's verdict resolve my angst. I don't like the idea of anyone being mad at me or doing anything to cause a woman frustration. "I need to focus. We've got a dog poisoner and a murderer on the loose. They could very well be the same person." I shoot

Marianne a sidelong glance. "I really wish this list of suspects would get smaller."

Marianne's mouth pulls to the side. "Nick and Nancy I would say are top of the list, if only because we have no other suspects."

"That's hardly a good reason."

Marianne shrugs. "The body was found in their home. Plus, the kitchen was spotless. That's not normal."

As much as I don't want to go there in my mind, there is no hiding the fact that Nick and Nancy very much did have a body shoved in their pantry—a body of someone they'd had a squabble with over a missing nutcracker.

I can only hope they knew nothing about the murder, and the true killer will unveil themselves soon.

7

BEING PART OF A TEAM

a knock sounds at the door, so Marianne moves to greet the guest while I finish plopping the batter into the liners. When I slide the pan into the oven, a smile finds my face when the sound of Logan's voice wafts through the house. "It's Thursday night," he announces as he comes in and takes off his coat. "That means your dishwasher is here. Running late, but here."

I greet Logan with a kiss on the cheek when he enters the kitchen. "It's good to see you. I know you're busy. It would have been okay if you couldn't come by tonight."

"Never too busy for you." He frowns at the sink. "I'm sorry, there is only one mountain of dishes in there. I'm used to two or three. You're making this too easy on me, ladies."

Marianne dumps a set of measuring cups and spoons into the sink to add to the pile. "Don't worry, we'll make it up to you." She moves to the notepad where she keeps a record of my recipes. She studies the ingredients before moving on to the next batch. "We were talking about how weird it was that Nick and Nancy had a whole giant meal for fifty going on in their kitchen, but the place was spotless."

I grimace at her solid logic. "Actually, there's more to that story. Helen has been making their Christmas feast for the past few years. Nick and Nancy wanted it kept secret so people could be impressed that they can do it all and entertain with a smile. But it's really Helen. She stopped by earlier that day around four o'clock and dropped off the already prepared food. She said the kitchen was in disarray when she arrived."

"Then they must have brought in the body and cleaned up after Helen left."

Logan takes off his uniform shirt, revealing a white undershirt that fits him perfectly. It's difficult not to stare. "That's a good theory." He kisses my cheek. "Miss Charlotte," he casts me a flirty smile that always manages to heat my features.

I set the timer on the oven. "Helen didn't open the pantry, so the body could have been there before she arrived." I shake my head. "It's not Nick and Nancy. I can't even picture Santa and Mrs. Claus murdering a man and shoving his body in a closet. It's not possible."

Marianne tilts her head in my direction. "It's entirely possible, but you don't want it to be true. Those are two very different things. Nick and Nancy could have cleaned up after Helen got there and before we arrived. There's a definite window of time that allots for it."

"But that doesn't make them guilty." I shake my head. "Helen mentioned that Nancy has a housekeeper, so that might solve the riddle of how the kitchen got cleaned up so quick without Nick and Nancy breaking a sweat."

Logan stills as the water runs over the dirty dishes. "What? Helen told you this?"

I nod, wondering what the controversy is in what I just said. "I saw Helen this morning."

His shoulders lower in defeat. "Nick and Nancy gave us a list of everyone who was in and out of the house that day. No housekeeper was mentioned."

"What does that mean?" Marianne inquires.

"Hopefully just that Nick and Nancy are getting on in years, and not that they are covering up for someone."

I grimace. "I feel like I said the wrong thing. I mean, Helen didn't say that the housekeeper was there, only that they have a housekeeper. I'll bet Nick and Nancy cleaned their own kitchen. That's the logical explanation, rather than hiring someone to clean a kitchen in half an hour and then split."

Logan shakes his head as he speaks. "You're right, I..."

I watch Logan's forearms tense as he picks up the mixing bowl and begins scrubbing it. Everything about him is perfection. He has a toned physique with a face that could make a model wallow in jealously. Kindness radiates off him without compromising his focus on a particular task. His sandy blond hair is perfectly parted. I never cared much about men's hair before, but now that I think about it, every man's hair pales in comparison with Logan's.

"Charlotte, did you hear me?" Logan asks, his chin dimple deepening as he gives me a wry look.

I didn't realize I was staring. "Oh, I..." But I never make it to a decent attempt at a fib to cover over my obvious ogling. My hand reaches out and knocks over a carton of eggs, spattering the sugar-speckled floor with a gooey mess. "Oh!" I drop to my knees, embarrassed that even after several dates and honest heart to heart conversations, Logan's handsome features still manage to turn me into a klutz. "I can't believe I did that."

Marianne's laughter spills out into the kitchen. "I love it! He asked you three times what you thought of the other guests' possible guilt, and you stared at him like he hadn't said a word. Then you... And the eggs... I love it! The Charlotte and Logan Show is my favorite thing to watch."

Logan grabs up a towel and kneels beside me, swiping at my chaos while I scoop the shells into the carton as best I can.

"I can't believe I did that. So embarrassing."

Logan smirks, clearly proud that he has such an effect on me still. "Good. I was starting to think I was losing my touch. You haven't spilled anything around me in a solid week."

I groan more at myself than the mess. "I'll get over it. It's the shirt."

Logan glances down at himself, his brow raising in question of my sanity, no doubt. "A white undershirt? That's what gets you going? I had no idea I was wearing something so scandalous."

I butt my forehead to his shoulder. "You wear it well," I admit, and then immediately regret how very forward I sound. I never say things like that. Compliments are different than the blatant hormonal ogling I just displayed. So embarrassing. "I need to go get the thing."

Marianne howls her amusement, doubled over with her hands on her knees. "What thing? What's so important that you have to run away from Logan, Charlotte?"

I know that if I stay near Logan a second longer, I am going to kiss him right in front of my best friend. Not just a peck or a sweet kiss, but a kiss laced with tongue and intention. So I do what any sane person would do.

Logan is a force of nature unto himself. Being in close quarters with him isn't something I am always prepared to handle gracefully.

I run outside and pretend I desperately need to check the mailbox.

I am not wearing a coat—a mistake I realize too late.

The chilly air picks up around me while I stand in front of the empty mailbox, hugging my bare arms and ruing the day I bought any and all short-sleeved shirts. I shiver as I stare into the shadowy box, chewing on my lower lip to conjure up a way to walk back into the house and play it off as if my actions just now were completely normal and not worth a conversation.

When the front door opens, I cover my face with my hands when I see Logan trotting out to me with my jacket in his hands. "You might need this," he tells me, fluttering my coat around my shoulders with the grace of a nobleman.

"Thanks. I..." But I don't know how to excuse my impulsivity.

The corner of Logan's mouth quirks upward. "Marianne is working on the frosting right now. I thought perhaps we could take a walk." He motions to the gray sky. "I never get to enjoy beautiful weather like this with anyone."

My exhale is filled with relief. Logan is too considerate a person to make me dig up a reason why I am ten years old when it comes to relationships. He proffers his arm to me like a true gentleman, waiting for me to zip my coat to start walking.

Our stroll is leisurely, despite the wind that might make smarter people want to hurry. "I haven't had much free time," he admits as we walk in step along the sidewalk. "This case has us all a little overwhelmed. There are so many people who had access to that house. I wish I could ask people questions and they would just answer honestly."

I grimace. "I didn't get Helen in trouble, did I? And Nick and Nancy aren't guilty. I'm sure of it."

"No one who is innocent will ever be in any trouble. They get added to the lengthy list of names we have to interview so we can get a larger picture of how Tom's body ended up in Nick and Nancy's pantry."

"Good luck with that. There were fifty people on the guest list."

Logan's shoulders fall in time with his steps slowing. "Are you serious? They only gave us forty-five names."

"Maybe a few people didn't show up," I suggest, worrying I am more firmly affixing the title of snitch on myself by accident.

"Maybe. This whole thing is such a headache. I can't even take the time to be sad that Tom is dead. There's too much paperwork and too many people to interview— some of whom could be lying. Nick and Nancy have a lot of holes in their story."

I cling tighter to him when a gust of icy wind stings our faces. "Did you know Tom well?" I can tell Logan needs to vent about his actual grief, rather than talk about the case that seems to be going nowhere.

"Tom was my little league coach."

An image of little boy Logan swims in my mind, complete with lopsided cap and jersey with a baseball bat in hand. "I didn't know you played baseball."

Logan's jacket is built for the weather, but he still shivers as he holds onto me. "Four years. Tom never had kids, so he was all in for helping us be a quality team. We kind of all felt like he was our summertime uncle. Sometimes he was the uncle who brings juice boxes and granola bars. Other times he was the uncle who gives you a stern talking to when you're being a jerk and need to grow up a little."

"That's sweet how involved he was."

Logan's jaw tightens, his eyes looking like he is seeing a distant memory instead of the cracked sidewalk stretching out in front of us. "I was picking on a kid one day at practice." He pauses for my intake of breath, but it never comes. "Really giving him a hard time. Tom pulled me aside and told me he was officially putting me in charge of protecting the kid I was terrorizing. That if anyone was mean to him, I would be the one to intercept it and make it stop. Said that he trusted me to be good to all the teammates." Logan shakes his head at his ten-year-old self. "Tom knew it was me who was hassling the kid. But he framed the situation in such a way that I realized I couldn't do that anymore. If I wanted to be on a team, I had to protect my teammates." Logan purses his lips while he thinks aloud. "Maybe that's a small life lesson, but I'm thirty-five years old, and I still remember it. Now that I'm on the force, I worry I'm not a good teammate when cases like this come up. When my dad locks himself in his office going over notes and interviews, trying to find the hole at the expense of his sanity, I feel so helpless. At least back in little league, I knew how to stop the bully, since I was the bully. I have no answers this time, and it's eating at me."

I don't rush to push aside his feelings, telling him how great he is when he is clearly convinced otherwise. "It sounds like you've got the weight of the precinct on your shoulders."

"Today I do. Might be like that for a while."

"Who looks out for you?"

Logan frowns, as if I have asked a confusing question. "What do you mean?"

"Who looks out for you? Who makes sure you don't work yourself sick, keeps you safe on the job and whatnot?"

"Wayne, my partner. My dad. Really everyone looks out for everyone."

"Then maybe more people than just you are looking out for your dad right now. Maybe it's not all on your shoulders after all. Isn't that one of the perks of being on a team?"

Logan's steps slow. "I guess that's true. I just hate that I can't solve this for my dad."

"Yet," I correct him. "You will. The team will."

Logan's arm drops so he can lace his fingers through mine. He stops walking and turns to face me in the fading evening light. Not even the gray clouds can disguise his beauty. Even in his sadness, Logan is a stunning sight. "Thanks. Sometimes I feel it all double. It's not just my boss, it's also my dad who's upset about this whole thing.

He and Tom are fishing buddies. He doesn't have time to grieve. Not while this case is unsolved. He wants to do a quality job on this investigation, but it's hard when you're mourning while everyone is lying to you, or at best telling half-truths."

"It sounds exhausting. Has he eaten today?"

Logan shakes his head. "I took him a sandwich this afternoon, but when I left, it was still untouched."

I lead our steps toward the house. "Then we're going to take a break from cupcakes and bring your dad some dinner." The thought of sitting with the intimidating sheriff ties my stomach in knots, but I know that's the right thing to do. "If we just drop off dinner, he won't take the time to eat it. But if we sit with him and have dinner together, we have a better chance of getting him to eat something."

Logan squeezes my hand, his steps picking up. "You would do that for him?"

"No," I admit. "But I would do that for you."

"I'll take it. What about your orders? You have a ton of cupcakes to bake."

"I'll finish the baking part, take food to your dad, then frost and package everything when I get back. It's fine."

When we reach the house, Logan stops on the porch steps, short of opening the front door. "Wait. I've been wanting to do this since I got here, but I know you're not a fan of public kissing."

My heart leaps into my throat when Logan takes my

face in his hands, thumbing at my cheeks before his mouth descends on mine. His lips are soft, and my only source of true warmth on this wintry December evening.

"Thank you for caring about my family," he whispers, his words caressing my lips between kisses.

I don't run from his beauty this time, though the thought isn't entirely dismissed from my mind. Instead, I lean in, savoring the sweetness this man brings me every time I am lucky enough to be the girl by his side.

8

CHICKEN AND RISOTTO

Though it was my idea to take dinner to the precinct for the sheriff, I regret my suggestion the second I step into the building. I know the sheriff isn't my biggest fan. We've never exactly hit it off. And now I am dating his son, which I'm sure he can't be too thrilled about. Plus, Aunt Winifred and the sheriff are always at odds, which doesn't help matters.

But this isn't about my hang-ups. This is about Logan's bleeding heart for his father, and a man's grief that hasn't had proper time to be aired out.

I keep my arms looped through the picnic basket, feeling foolish and childish strolling through the empty precinct. The place is usually closed in the evening, but there is one sheriff who isn't ready to go home for the day.

I stand by Logan's side when he tries the handle of his father's office and finds it locked. He knocks on the door, keeping up the rhythm until his dad opens it, poking his head out with a frown. "What's going on, Logan?"

Instead of standing outside the office, Logan politely pushes his way inside, forcing his father to have a conversation he cannot shut out with a simple slam of a door. "Hey, Dad." His eyes fall on the untouched sandwich on the desk that now should probably be thrown away. "I thought maybe you'd skipped lunch, so we brought you dinner."

"We?" The sheriff's eyes fall on me, standing in the doorway with my picnic basket still on my arm. His brows knit together, clearly as enthusiastic about spending time together as I am. "I don't have time for this, Logan."

"You don't have time to eat? Are you on the verge of a breakthrough in the case?"

"No, but that's why..."

"Good. Then you have time to sit down and eat something." Logan starts shuffling papers into piles and moving them to the side, so we have a space to spread out the food. "We made risotto and roasted chicken with salad."

The sheriff runs his hand over his face. "You made what?"

"You heard me, old man." Logan rolls his eyes. "Fine. Charlotte made it, but I helped. I can chop vegetables and stir things in pans."

That's debatable, to be honest. Yes, he can chop things, but risotto has to be constantly stirred, and Logan likes to talk with his hands, so the rice stuck to the pan more than once. But still, the risotto turned out just fine, and chicken is hard to screw up, so that should be good enough to fill the sheriff's empty belly.

The sheriff shoots me what can only be described as a friendly glower when he realizes we aren't going to be ignored, and neither will his growling stomach. "I see you've got my son cooking. I admit, I didn't think that was possible. He only makes pizzas and sandwiches."

Logan mimes a laugh. "Hilarious. I'm not completely inept."

The sheriff sighs, surrendering his protest that he cannot take a break to eat. He sits in his chair, leaving Logan and I to take the guest chairs on the other side of his desk. "Well, this is quite the spread. To what do I owe the pleasure?"

Logan and I take out the food and cutlery while he voices his concerns to his father. "You're not eating. Judging by the bags under your eyes, you're not sleeping. I know this would be a hard case, even if you weren't close to Tom. But being that you two are friends, it's that much easier to throw yourself into work and forget the basics, like sustenance."

The sheriff leans back in his chair as he pops the top off his travel plate. "This is thoughtful but not necessary. I'll eat when I'm hungry."

Logan doubles down. "Actually, you'll eat when my girlfriend and I bring you a meal that we made for you. I don't care if it's chopped liver and beets, you'll clean your plate and swear up and down that it's the best meal you've ever had."

The sheriff chuckles at being put in his place by his son. "I guess that's not too tall an order." He meets my eyes with a glimmer of sincerity. "Thank you. This is nice."

I'll believe it when he takes the first bite. As it is, he picks up his fork and merely pushes the food around in the container.

Logan digs into his, having been taunted by the smell of the food while it was cooking. "How has Mom taken to you giving up showering?"

The sheriff rolls his eyes at his son. "I've been busy."

"I can see that. But Tom's killer isn't likely to turn himself or herself in if you smell bad enough to scare people away. You know, I'll bet that's what the culprit has been waiting for. Too grossed out to come and turn themselves in."

The sheriff mimes a laugh, looking much like Logan with the wry tilt of his head. "Hilarious." He sets his plate down, the food untouched. "I feel like I'm failing Tom, letting his killer walk around this long without seeing justice. He was killed in his own home with one of his own kitchen knives, by the way. We discovered that when we went to his house. But other than those clues, there was no evidence left behind at his house as to who might have done it. I can't imagine who would do something like that to someone like him." He shakes his head. "Guess I'll be cancelling the ice fishing trip I had planned to take with him next month."

Logan's green eyes steel. "Don't cancel it. I'll go with you. We'll catch one for Tom. Maybe it'll be such a huge fish that he'll feel the need to come back and haunt us just to get a good look at it."

The sheriff chortles at what is the most macabre joke I have heard in quite some time. But the two of them have a comfortable back and forth, using their unique brand of humor to soothe over the pain of the week.

The sheriff leans his elbow on his armrest and fixes his stare my way. "It's hard to believe my Logan has finally found someone he likes enough to bring around me. If you can get your crazy aunt to stop getting into shenanigans, I'll be convinced you're a miracle worker."

I display my untouched food to him. "I'll settle for getting you to eat, instead of pushing that food around on your plate."

The corner of the sheriff's mouth quirks up. "You're a tough one. Good. You can keep my boy in line."

"Hey, hey," Logan protests, but the outside of his shoe taps to mine, and then he links his ankle around mine to further tether us together.

I don't eat a thing until the sheriff takes two bites of his food. Relief fills the air when the sheriff sighs at the flavor of the risotto paired with the chicken breast. "This is good. Maybe I did need to eat something after all."

Logan shovels his mouth full of food. "I'll settle for a simple, 'Logan, you were right, and I was wrong.'"

"Let's not get carried away."

The conversation quickly turns back to the unsolved case, since that is where both men's minds are stuck. "Charlotte overheard something interesting," Logan tells his father. "Nick and Nancy have a housekeeper. We need to ask them if their housekeeper was at the house the day of the party. That's a detail that might have been missed."

The sheriff groans. "Honestly, it's like one lie after another with this couple. I like Nick and Nancy as much as the next guy, but I've never seen two people try to cover up the silliest things. Not telling us that Helen was at the house because Nancy was embarrassed people might find out she didn't cook the meal herself? What does that have to do with anything? If I find out a housekeeper was cleaning after I specifically asked them for a complete list of people who'd been in and out of the house that day, I'm going to lose my temper. Why is Nancy's flimsy pride more important than investigating a man's death?"

Logan shrugs. "Beats me. But all these rabbit trails are worth looking into."

"I'll add the housekeeper to the lengthy list." The sheriff takes a few more bites, nearly halfway finished with his meal with no further prodding needed on our part.

"And Charlotte mentioned that Nancy told her fifty people were supposed to be at the party, but only forty-five were on the list she gave us."

I chime in with my earlier point. "But perhaps people sent in an RSVP without showing up. That happens."

"True," the sheriff said. "I got the list of invites and matched them against the people who showed up and started making those calls this afternoon. You're right, Charlotte, five weren't at the party."

Logan shakes his head. "You're on top of things. You need a shower, but you're on top of work, at least."

"Hey, one victory at a time." I love that they aren't putting on classy guest conversation for my benefit. They're not even withholding police talk from me, which I appreciate. It's like they don't mind having me in their space. "I spoke to Dennis and Laura today. They were supposed to come but one of their kids came down with the flu, so they stayed home. I couldn't get ahold of the three other people who didn't make it to the party, so I'm going to stop by their homes tomorrow to get their statements of where they were that night, starting with Marcus McManus."

Logan shakes his head. "You know Marcus hates talking to the police. He's not going to tell you a thing, even if he's completely innocent, which I'm sure he is."

The sheriff slumps in his seat. "I know, but cooperative or not, I have to do my due diligence."

I didn't realize how much work went into investigating a case. I raise my hand as if I am in class when the name they are discussing rings a bell. "Actually, Marcus McManus ordered a dozen cupcakes from me. He's coming to pick them up tomorrow. What do you need to ask him, other than why he didn't go to the party?"

The sheriff casts me a wary look but doesn't clam up. "That's basically it. Finding out if Marcus had some sort of beef with Tom is a bonus, but not completely necessary. None of the five people who didn't show up to the party are actual suspects. But when we have no leads, we have to look under every rock."

Logan's brows knit together. "I'll come over and hang out in the kitchen with you tomorrow morning, just in case things get hostile."

I tilt my head at him. "I thought you just said that Marcus hates talking to the police. On the clock or not, he's not going to do a whole lot of talking if you're at my house. I thought the point was to cross him off the list of suspects. I can make small talk just as well as the next person, and that seems to be all it'll take."

The sheriff examines me with an appraising look. "You know, she's not wrong. Plus, I need you here in the morning to help me get through the actual suspects, Logan. You sure you don't mind, Charlotte?"

"I offered. I'm seeing Marcus anyway when he comes to pick up the cupcakes. If I can't work it organically into the conversation, then I won't. Either way, you'll be no worse off if I try."

The sheriff stabs his chicken and shoves a bite into his mouth. "Thanks, kiddo. I appreciate it. I'm up to my ears with this case. There's a lot of information to sift through, and there's no way of telling which bits are important."

I can tell Logan doesn't like this one bit, but he's too grateful that his father and I are getting along to protest me doing a little poking around in my spare time. "Nothing that could put you in a vulnerable state, okay? The first whiff that you get of this guy being the tiniest bit guilty, you slam the door shut and lock him out. Sound fair?"

"Sounds like you care about me." Though it's a bold statement to make—especially in front of his father—I don't hold back my words.

Logan's smile eases any tension that's been building in the room. "You know I do."

The sheriff examines us with a small smile dimpling his chin. Though I know he's got a lot on his plate and even more on his mind, I can tell he is pleased at the sight of his son bringing someone in so we can all have dinner together.

Though I played off making small talk with Marcus McManus as no big deal, now I am determined to do my best so the sheriff doesn't have to worry that I can't keep up with his son.

9

CUPCAKE FLIRTING

I have been close to silent as I cleaned up the kitchen and the living room this morning. Winifred made it home safely from her trip to have a relaxing vacation and see the nude ice sculpture exhibit with Karen and Agnes. I want to make sure she sleeps in without interruption. I take my time fixing waffles that she can pop in the toaster to reheat once she wakes up. Then I brew her some coffee to help set her back on her normal morning routine.

One good thing about the three of them being out of town the day Tom's body was discovered is that the Live Forever Club is not on the sheriff's list of suspects. Though, I know if he could find a way to include them on that sheet, he would.

I get the cupcake boxes ready, lining them up in alphabetical order to make for a more seamless pickup.

When people start arriving at nine o'clock, I am ready for each one to be Marcus McManus. By the fifth pickup, I'm starting to get texts from Logan, asking me if I am alright and if I need him to come over for backup.

I text back a message to let him know that nothing at all has happened that is worth worrying about. A conversation between two innocent people never requires backup. Still, I know he won't relax until the casual interview is over.

When Lisa Swanson comes to the front door, I greet her with a hug. She is the woman who wrote out the business plan that allowed me to quit my job waitressing at Bill's Diner so I could open up my cupcake bakery out of the house. Though we've had our ups and downs, the fact that her name was on my list of orders this week made me happy.

"It's good to see you, Lisa," I say after I release her from my hug. "How are you?"

She casts me a wan smile as she adjusts the knitted hat on her head. "Oh, you know. Single life is strange after being married for so many years, but I'm okay. Found a new gym that I like, so that's been helpful."

"That's great. Anywhere nearby?"

But I don't fully tune into her reply because the next person who comes to call waves at us through the glass door. "Pickup for Marcus McManus!" he sings cheerily.

My eyes widen and my smile turns forced. "Come on in." I wave the tall and wiry man inside, making it seem like I always welcome people into the home rather than meeting them at the door with their order. "I'm Charlotte. We haven't formally met."

"Actually, we sort of did. You came through my Spook Booth at the Halloween Festival. I was the one stabbing the zombie through the chest." His eyes go wide as he bares his teeth, miming a sickening stabbing motion that looks suspiciously close to what may have happened to Tom to end his life prematurely.

That is not evidence of guilt, I remind myself. *That is merely theatrics.*

I shake his hand and usher him inside. "Lisa, do you know Marcus?"

Lisa bats her hand his way. "Of course. We go way back. Good to see you, Marcus."

He dons a sympathetic head tilt, his short brown hair angling to the side. "It's good to see you out and about. I'm real sorry to hear about Wesley and that whole business." He picks up his box of cupcakes and taps the lid. "I'm having a movie night at my house tomorrow at six. Feel like being social?"

Lisa's mouth pops open, clearly unused to people being nice to her for no reason. The rumors around Sweetwater Falls were that she was cheating on her husband Wesley with her personal trainer. When that turned out to be the furthest thing from the truth, I think the townspeople realized how self-serving their gossip was, especially after Wesley was found out to be the real problem in their marriage.

Now that she is single and clearly not a cheater, I keep waiting for people to finally open their hearts to her. Perhaps Marcus will be the start of that.

Lisa bobs on the balls of her feet. "That sounds great. You sure you don't mind?"

His smile is genuine. "You might be the one rethinking the invitation when you hear the movie choice."

"Don't tell me," she replies, sheer delight playing on her features. "I want to be surprised."

I love that I get to be a fly on the wall for this moment. I know nothing about Marcus, but I am so happy that he has taken the leap to get Lisa out of her house and around people again.

It's then that I remember my mission.

"I can't put my finger on where I saw you last, other than the Spook Booth. Were you at Nick and Nancy's Christmas party? Maybe I saw you there."

A weird sort of grimace contorts his features. "No. I was invited but I didn't end up going. Good thing, I guess. Poor Tom. Whoever stabbed him through the chest and stuffed him in the pantry is sick."

If Marcus wasn't at the party, how would he know a detail like that?

I push further into the topic. "Shame you missed seeing Nick and Nancy's house all decorated, though. It was beautiful."

He shrugs noncommittally. "I'll catch it next year."

"What'd you end up doing instead?"

"Just stayed home. Some days I'm up for going out, while other days it's a good night to stay in."

"All by yourself?" I ask, prying more than I normally would because I know the sheriff will want to know if anyone can corroborate his story.

"Well, not all by myself. My golden retriever kept me company."

Drat. Marcus is still on the list of suspects, then, because as good a companion his dog may be, it's not enough to erase suspicion that Marcus may have had a reason for wanting to distance himself from the party that night.

He holds his box of cupcakes in one hand and fiddles with his keys in the other. "Nick and Nancy are great, but I just wasn't feeling it that day. I think I'm overcommitting. My goal is to keep things low-key this season. I'll go to the Christmas Festival, but I'm not running my usual booth. Too much work."

Lisa dons a mild pout. "Oh, really? That's a shame. I love your Christmas booth." She loops her arm through mine. "Every year, Marcus has a Decorate Your Own Sugar Cookie booth. It's so sweet. The kids are always lined up to use the pretty sprinkles he brings."

The corner of Marcus' mouth quirks. "I didn't realize the adults paid attention to the details."

Lisa blinks at him, a demure smile on her face. "I noticed."

"I would do the booth, but it's a lot of work to make it all happen by myself. I'm not getting any younger." This must be his attempt at a joke, because he looks to be around Logan's age.

Lisa twirls a lock of her blonde hair around her finger, her hip cocking to the side. "If you're looking for a helper, I'd be happy to do something like that with you. It sounds like fun."

The corner of his mouth twitches. "I wouldn't mind that in the least. Might just give me back some of that Christmas spirit I've been missing out on so far this year."

Watching them flirt and make plans gives me a giddy lightness in my chest, but I'm starting to feel like the third wheel. I hope they leave together so they can continue this cuteness outside.

Her head tilts to the side. "No Christmas spirit for you? Marcus, that's sad."

He shrugs his sinewy shoulders. "Just going through a funk, I guess. But now I'm actually looking forward to the Christmas festival. Who knew all I needed was someone to crack jokes with at the booth and that would solve it all?"

I hand Lisa's box of cupcakes to Marcus. "Would you mind carrying Lisa's box to her car for her?" I don't bother making up a reason why a woman who goes to the gym multiple times a week, eats healthy and has like, zero body fat might need assistance carrying a three-pound box. It's starting to look like they will jump on the flimsiest excuse to spend more time together.

I love it.

I watch them walk down the path to their vehicles, talking and smiling the whole way. Even though I couldn't get the answers I'm sure the sheriff was hoping for, I'm glad I got to be there when a conversation between two old friends became a spark of possibly something more.

UNBALANCED

*L*isa's call to me on Saturday morning is a welcome surprise.

"We talked all afternoon, Charlotte! Not a span of awkward silence, either. I'm going to his house tonight for the movie night with his friends, but we also made plans to go to a restaurant in Hamshire tomorrow afternoon, just the two of us!"

It's so good to hear Lisa's joy bubbling out of her. After her split with Wesley, I was sure she would remain isolated for a long time. Marcus looked to be a good decade and a half younger than her, so the match is a bit of a head turner, to be sure. But hey, if she's happy, then I hope they go on many more dates together.

"That's awesome, Lisa. He seems like a nice guy." Actually, I have no idea what he seems like. We had three minutes of conversation in which I couldn't verify his whereabouts during a murder.

Lisa chats on and on about Marcus' good points, filling me in on the details of their banter yesterday and what it could all be leading toward. Before I moved to Sweetwater Falls, I didn't have a single friend who called me up just to talk about their day. I love how enmeshed the people in Sweetwater Falls are in each other's lives.

It makes me think of Tom, and wonder who was in his life so much that they would notice if he was in some sort of trouble. Who did he call up to share his day-to-day details?

He went fishing with the sheriff.

He lived next door to Delia. Though they don't seem like they were close friends but more passive enemies.

Tom wasn't invited to Nick and Nancy's party, yet someone thought to stash his body at their house. What's the connection between the Christmastime couple and Tom?

Lisa is still talking about what a great date she had. This gives me plenty of time to sort out my thoughts on the matter that's been bothering me for nearly a week now. I need to talk with Nick and Nancy to see if there is any reason why their house was chosen for Tom's body to be stashed there.

Lisa and I end our call twenty minutes later. I'm glad she has a date lined up for the night. I, on the other hand, have business details to tend to. Once a week, Marianne has me balance the books. That's really something she is better suited for, but it's good medicine for me to learn the ins and outs of how my business functions.

I start with taking inventory, making a list of any ingredients I will need to purchase for next week's orders. Then I open up the online banking for the business and balance the receipts, making sure each payment cleared for the cupcakes that went out yesterday.

I frown as I make my list and check it twice. Three times. Four.

The books aren't balancing.

My mouth pulls to the side as I go over each transaction, crossing it off the list I have going of every order that was placed in the past week. It's odd, but the number is way off.

When I narrow in on the payment that is missing, I start to chew on my lower lip.

Nick and Nancy's check didn't clear. They paid half prior to book the job, and gave me a check for the other half upon completion, which I cashed the following day.

I lean my elbows on the table, grinding my knuckles into my temples. I reach for my phone and call Marianne, who I know is in hour two of her shift at the library. "Remind me why I thought I could be a decent businesswoman," I say in lieu of a greeting.

Marianne chuckles at my fretting. "Because you are a good businesswoman. Tell me what's wrong, and we'll solve it together."

"The books aren't balancing because Nick and Nancy's check bounced. Now I have to call them up and tell them they have to resend the payment, which will be so awkward."

"It will be awkward for them, Charlotte. You didn't do anything wrong. The fact that you're balancing your books regularly means you are doing the right thing. Call them up and politely tell them the issue. I'm sure it'll be no big deal."

I close my eyes. "I could always let it slide. They've got a lot on their plate right now."

Marianne's voice turns stern. "Don't even consider it. I'm going to call you in one hour, Charlotte McKay. You're going to have touched base with them. I mean it. We're not going to be The Pushover Bakers: Pay if You Feel Like It. We're a serious business who does good work. You deserve to be paid."

I hang my head, my stomach churning as I digest the good medicine that is Marianne's wisdom. "I know you're right. For the record, I hate this part."

"You would be a monster if you loved it. But this is what owning a business is some days. You can do it. Charlotte the Brave, right?"

I groan, because nothing inside of me feels brave right now. I want to crawl under a blanket and hide from my responsibilities.

Marianne's voice turns grave. "You have one hour."

I snort at her impression of a hostage negotiator. "Fine, fine. Stop being good at everything. It's intimidating."

Marianne's smile is evident in her reply. "I can't help it. Talk to you soon."

When we end the call, I clunk my forehead to the table, banging it three times because I really, really don't want to have this conversation with two people who are already under a ton of stress.

Still, I know if I put this off even five minutes, Marianne will somehow know. If it was just me I was letting down by chickening out, that would be one thing, but Marianne has put numerous hours of hard work into the business. She doesn't deserve to work for The Pushover Bakers: Pay if You Feel Like It. She deserves to take pride in the Bravery Bakery: specializing in the world's best honey cakes.

Winifred's voice trails into the kitchen. "She's right, you know. Call them. It won't be as bad as you're thinking." Her fingernails trill along my nape, relaxing a modicum of my tension.

"Oh, fine." I sit up. "Hey, you never filled me in on the high points of your trip. I want to hear all about it."

Winifred chortles as she sits down at the table beside me, tying her silver curls back with a yellow bow. "I'll tell you everything after you make that phone call and get your money."

I stick my tongue out at her, but comply because she's right and I am being a chicken.

This is torture.

I pick up the phone, putting it on speaker when Winifred taps her ear to let me know she wants in on the conversation. "Hello, Nancy. This is Charlotte McKay. Do you have a minute?"

"A minute, yes. What can I do for you, sweetheart?"

I can feel my palms starting to sweat. "There seems to a small problem with... um... See I was balancing the books and it seems your check might have bounced." I squinch my eyes shut, wishing I could pawn this particularly dreadful task off onto anyone else.

"What?"

If she makes me say it again, I might cry.

Nancy's tone comes with a forced lightness. "You might need to look again, honey. There's no way the check bounced. There is plenty of money in our accounts."

Winifred gives me a bolstering look, her round chin firming.

"I looked at the bank statement, and it's saying that your check was returned due to insufficient funds."

Nancy's voice turns to ice. "What exactly are you insinuating? Do you think we can't afford a few cupcakes? And let me just say what poor form it is for you to be calling me to ask for money. No one barely touched the desserts because the police cleared out the party before dinner was even served."

My cheeks are hot and my voice squeaky. "I'm not

trying to insult you, Nancy. I can come by and pick up my payment later today. How does noon sound?"

"It sounds pushy. I don't think I should have to pay twice for cupcakes nobody ate once."

It's a hit to my pride to picture my hard work ending up in her trash, but I can't help that.

Winifred's upper lip curls at the phone. She makes a fist, reminding me not to back down. Her sea green eyes meet my blue ones, reminding me silently to be brave.

"I'm only asking you to pay once, Nancy. I'll see you at noon. Thanks for understanding." I end the call before it can get any uglier. I hold my great-aunt's gaze. "Is it okay if I throw up now?"

11

THE SHAKEDOWN

*W*inifred's chin lifts after I end the call with Nancy. "You handled that beautifully. Like a true business owner. Some people will always try to get out of paying for things. You can't let their hang-ups become yours. You did the right thing. You deserve to be paid."

"I'm going to print out the statement that shows her check bounced, just so she knows I'm not trying to get paid twice for one job."

"Do what you need to keep your head high, but she already knows you're not scamming her. Nancy's just being difficult because clearly they are having money problems." Winifred shakes her head. "I wouldn't have guessed, being that they always have nice things, drive a pricey car and have lavish parties, but I guess you never know what goes on behind closed doors."

I massage my temples. "I don't want to know what goes on behind closed doors. I want to be paid and not think about their party ever again."

Winifred sets her elbow on the table. "Then I guess this is a bad time to ask if you want to talk about Tom's body falling on you."

I squint at her. "Very bad time. I'd rather hear about your trip. Tell me everything."

"Well, I'll only tell you the parts suitable for young ears. We had a marvelous time. The boardwalk view was spectacular. At night, it's completely deserted. We did some moonlight painting one of the nights. So inspiring to have a change of scenery."

"I cannot imagine scenery more inspiring than the landscape of Sweetwater Falls, but then again, I'm still known around town as 'the new girl'."

Winifred regales me with stories of their trip, complete with showing me pictures from her phone of the three of them going on a chilly ferry ride and a few blurry shots of the nude ice sculptures.

I love listening to her life. While we drink tea and trade giggles, my tension begins to ease. I love living with Aunt Winnie. She makes everything better.

By the time noon approaches, I feel as if I was along for her trip, knowing each detail that made her smile. She has a beautiful smile, and one that she puts to good use often, so as not to deprive the world of her joy.

"Shall we?" Winifred inquires, standing and rinsing out her teacup.

"We? You don't want to come along to hear Nancy tap dance her way around paying me again. It's embarrassing for both parties."

Winifred grabs the key to her golf cart. "I'll drive. We'll be nice and chilly from the ride, so we won't be as likely to fold."

"I fail to see the logic in hypothermia making a person bolder."

"Easy. We'll be anxious to get back home, so we'll be firmer about getting paid and leaving."

"Oh, good. I was hoping to be extra confrontational."

Winifred winks at me. "That's what I'm here for."

We bundle up with extra scarves and mittens and then get into the golf cart, which was clearly built with warmer weather in mind. The icy air pelts at our faces, stinging our cheeks to ask us why on earth we chose this vehicle to travel eight miles in when I have a perfectly good sedan with a heater sitting in the garage.

By the time we get to Nick and Nancy's house, I am so cold, there is no chance I will not make this visit brief. I want to get home and into a hot bath as soon as humanly possible. I knock on the door with Winifred by my side. She has the look of thrill about her because she loves when I am forced to face my fears.

"You can do it," Winifred reminds me. "Remember,

Nancy's protests have nothing to do with you. She's mad at herself, not at you. Don't let her bully you into folding."

"I'm too cold to debate with her. I'm taking the money and getting out of here."

Winifred grins at me, tapping her temple with her gloved finger. "See? Brilliant, isn't it. The cold is a good motivator not to dawdle."

"It's also a good motivator not to drive in a golf cart in the early stages of winter."

When the door opens, Nick greets us with a jolly smile. "To what do I owe the pleasure, ladies? Come on in. Did I know you were coming?" He pats my shoulder and leans in so he can kiss Winifred's cheek. Even clad in a Christmas sweater and black trousers, he looks like an off-duty Santa Claus, complete with the twinkle in his eyes.

I groan internally that I am about to shake down Santa Claus for loose change.

I don't come in further than the foyer. "Hi, Nick. I told Nancy we would be here at noon." I skip over my hemming and hawing and go right for the blatant truth. "The check you gave me for the cupcakes didn't clear, so I told her I would come for the payment at noon. Am I early?"

Nick's eyes widen. "Oh, I had no idea. Sorry about that. Must be an oversight in my old age. Let me get some cash. Hold on. How much was it for?"

Nancy comes around the corner, a frown firmly fixed

on her face. "Nick, we already paid them half. And the guests barely ate any of the cupcakes. The money we paid should more than cover the cost of the ingredients."

Nick frowns at his wife. "I don't see how that matters. It's not Charlotte's fault a dead body fell on her and ruined the party. She held up her end of the bargain. It's only right we hold up ours."

Nancy guffaws. "Still, it's ridiculous. We already paid her!"

"She's saying the check bounced."

Nancy's mouth firms before her voice comes out at a shrill shout, making me jump. "We are missing four nutcrackers! Four! That's more than any other year. I'm not giving her a cent until she returns what she stole."

Whiskers pokes her head around the corner, watching us surreptitiously to see if there's anything good in the way of human entertainment today.

Winifred barks out a laugh, even though I cannot possibly see what might be funny about this situation.

Nancy straightens sanctimoniously, glaring at my great-aunt. "Is something amusing, Winifred?"

"You think my niece stole one of your nutcrackers? For what? How could you possibly think she would want one of those creepy things? And how much does one cost? Ten dollars?"

Nancy harrumphs. "I will have you know that one of the nutcrackers that was stolen was purchased for three hundred dollars this summer. It's a one-of-a-kind collector's item, hand painted and signed by the artist. If Charlotte stole that, then she owes us far more than we owe her."

Winifred covers her mouth. "You spent three hundred dollars on a nutcracker, yet you're about to short my niece on payments for goods she most certainly delivered? I'll never understand you, Nancy." She tilts her head to the side, sizing up Nancy. "Then again, maybe I understand you completely."

I get the feeling that there is more to their friendship than I am aware of.

Nancy wags her finger at Aunt Winifred. "You always were jealous of me. Of my house. Of my marriage. Of my things. I don't need to apologize for my wealth, Winnie! Certainly not to you."

Whoa. This conversation is taking a weird turn.

Nick's cheeks turn pink. "Nancy, you know that's not relevant. Winnie and I dated decades ago, long before you and I even met."

It's my turn to hold in a laugh at the scandal. I guess there is more to the story than I realized.

Winifred smirks at Nancy, which I'm guessing is going to make steam pour out of Nancy's ears in the next minute if we can't diffuse this argument quickly. "The only thing you need to apologize for is thinking you could not pay my niece and then shame her for it. I don't care how many useless baubles you fill your home with. I like when you're happy, Nancy. But it doesn't look to me like you're the least bit relaxed today." She motions around the home. "You brought this conversation upon yourself. Now if you'll just pay us, we'll be out of your hair."

I fret at the blatant accusation, my upper lip sweating. "I didn't steal your nutcrackers, Nancy. Honestly, I don't want to upset you. I only came here to get paid. I'm sure it's not an issue with your account. I'm sure the bank just made a mistake."

I'm not sure about any of that, but it's the most polite excuse I can think to give.

Aunt Winifred's derisive scoff isn't entirely helpful, nor is it unexpected.

Nancy's shoulders roll back, slightly mollified. "I supposed that's a possibility. Because I know how to balance a checkbook, young lady. I've been balancing my checkbook longer than you've been alive!"

I hold up my hands. "I have no doubt. I only came here to get paid. I even printed out the statement for you, so you would know I'm not trying to swindle you." I hand the folded sheet of paper to Nick, hating that my word isn't enough.

He frowns, looking it over. "Huh. Yep, looks like we owe you a bit of money. Sorry about that, Charlotte. I hope you'll cater our party next year. Such a sad affair. I love Christmas. To have something so tragic happen at our Christmas party? I'm still not over it."

My whole demeanor softens. "None of us are over it. I'm so sorry you lost your friend. Did you know Tom well?"

Nick holds his hand out and tilts it from side to side. "As well as anybody, I guess. Such a shame. I can't imagine why anyone would want to hurt him. Talked to him not too long ago. Nice fella."

"What did you two talk about?"

Nick chuckles, his belly shaking enough to make him truly look the part of Santa Claus. "Oh, nothing interesting. Just how bad we both are at keeping house." He motions around himself to his lavish home. "This doesn't happen overnight, you know."

"You do a great job. Your house was spotless at the Christmas party."

"Thank you, young lady. That day, Nancy and I can take credit for. We wanted the housekeeper to come over and clean the morning of the party, but she wasn't available. So we rolled up our sleeves and did it ourselves." He flexes a muscle and grants me a small smile.

I guess that crosses the housekeeper off the list of suspects.

Nick tugs out his wallet and hands me a few bills. I make to pocket them without counting, but Winifred takes the money from my hand to double check that we won't need to come back here and have this awkward conversation all over again.

"I'm so sorry Tom passed. Do the police have any leads?"

Nancy frowns at me. "They think we had something to

do with it. As if we could carry a grown man into our house and shove him in our pantry. The nerve."

Winifred puts her hand on my arm. "I'm sure the guilty party will be brought to light soon enough. Have a good afternoon, Nick. Nancy."

We make our way outside, leaving the tension behind us with the slam of a door.

My brow raises at my great-aunt. "You must be incredibly hard to get over, you minx. What was that about?"

Winifred smirks, looking all smug as she leads the way to her golf cart. "A respectable lady never kisses and tells. Fortunately, I gave up being a respectable lady years ago, so I have no qualms telling you that Nick and I dated shortly before he met Nancy."

"Who ended it? You or Nick?"

Winifred slides into the golf cart, waiting for me to take my seat beside her. "Who even remembers a detail like that? It was two decades ago." She casts me a sidelong glance laced with mischief and a little pride. "I ended it. I've never been one for long-term relationships. In truth, I was grateful Nancy came along. Nick used to follow me around like a lovesick pup before she caught his eye." She starts up the cart and putters us down the road. "But those sorts of things hardly matter this many years later."

"Apparently they matter to Nancy. Did you see how livid she looked to have you in her house?"

A true self-satisfied grin spreads over my great-aunt's face. "We came there to get your payment, which we did.

The fact that Nancy lost her mind over seeing me in her home? That's just the icing on the cupcake, my dear."

Despite the chilly air pelting our cheeks, we laugh together as Winifred tells me her tawdry tales of the man she left far, far behind.

12

A BRAVE MISSTEP

*W*hen Lisa Swanson invites Marianne and me out for coffee and chit-chat, I am pleased to accept. We haven't had honest to goodness girl time in months, so this is a welcome note on my calendar. When I pull into The Snuggle Inn, a coziness falls over me even before I am greeted by the warmth of the building's heater. I have fond memories of hanging out with Fisher in the kitchen here, dropping off my cupcakes when I used to bake for The Snuggle Inn so Fisher could concentrate on his true passion: handmade pasta and fancy dinners.

Entering the inn with a box of cupcakes under my arm is nothing new. I always bring Fisher a treat when I visit.

But this box is filled with intention. With a proposal. With hope.

I didn't tell Marianne, Logan or the Live Forever Club that I reserved extra cupcakes from the orders I filled last night. I tried my hardest not to think my plan through, other than placing a phone call to the new owner of The Snuggle Inn yesterday to schedule a meeting before my coffee date with Marianne and Lisa. I know that if I think about how much I want to be selling my cupcakes at a restaurant, I will chicken out and remember that things like this have not always been a success for me in the past. I've had the misfortune of choosing two businesses whose owners were less than reputable, so the contracts dissolved after only a handful of weeks.

But Lenny is the new owner of The Snuggle Inn, and even though earlier this year there wasn't enough money in their budget to outsource cupcake baking to me, perhaps things have changed for them, making them open to the idea.

Perhaps Lenny just needs to try one of my cupcakes, and he will be convinced that he absolutely must have my desserts on the menu.

I am brave. I am brave. I can do this.

I chant my pep talk over and over in my mind, cheering myself on because I was too chicken to tell my usual cheerleaders that I was going to be stepping out on uneven business terrain this morning.

This needs to be *my* thing. I need to be brave without a cheering section.

Or I could cancel the meeting, and no one would ever know.

The thought to ditch is tempting, but I've come this far.

Might as well see how far taking a leap for my business will get me.

I don't beeline for the kitchen as I usually do to greet Fisher. Instead, I wait at the front desk, smiling at the receptionist and requesting she tell Lenny I am here for our eleven o'clock meeting.

My palms are sweaty, so much that I worry I will leave wet marks on the pink box, so I set it on the reception desk. When a man in his forties comes around the corner wearing a white dress shirt and navy trousers, his black hair slicked to the side with a bit too much gel, I smile at him in lieu of offering to shake his hand. "Hi, Lenny. Thanks for meeting with me."

He jerks his chin toward the hallway to the left. "Hi, Charlotte. You can come to my office."

I follow him, so nervous now that I begin to question every step I took that led me to this meeting. What was I thinking, pitching my cupcakes to a business without Marianne or the Live Forever Club looking over my numbers? I am using their standard equation of charging three times more than what it costs to make them, but I didn't double-check anything with them. Should I charge less because Lenny is a new owner? Should I have Karen here to look over any sort of contract, so I don't agree to something devious that might be hidden in the fine print?

I am so nervous that I don't look at what I am setting the cupcake box down on. I realize too late that the stack of papers is tilting the box. I move to correct my mistake, but my hand is clumsy. Instead of scooting the box to a clear spot on the desk, I knock the entire thing to the floor, smashing the cupcakes on their heads and utterly shattering my chances at securing this job.

Lenny gapes at me. "I guess this is going to be a shorter meeting than I anticipated." He checks his phone. "It's just as well. All the rooms are booked and the social director is out sick, so I'm filling in for her."

I gape at the horror of my carefully crafted cupcakes on the floor. The only good thing is that the lid managed to stay secured on the box, so there isn't a sugary mess to clean up off the carpet.

"I'm so sorry. I'm happy to come back another time and show you what I can really do." My pitch comes out in a spluttery gust. "I've worked with The Snuggle Inn before. I never was late with a delivery and my cupcakes sold out every time. Fisher and I work well together, so I'm not stepping on any toes. I brought my price sheet!" I flutter out the page and slap it on the table, then crouch down to pick of my box of cupcakes, along with my destroyed pride.

Lenny glances at the sheet out of pure politeness. "These are a little pricey. I think we're going to have to pass. Even though The Snuggle Inn is an established business, the whole model of how we run things now is different, so luxuries like overpriced cupcakes aren't in the budget at this time."

My stomach drops as I fight the urge to lower my prices

on the spot. I have utterly blown this interview and am no closer to getting my cupcakes sold at a restaurant.

I hang my head while everything in me weights itself with shame. This was too big a leap. I should have listened to that voice inside of me that said not to try anything like this.

Play it safe.

There's nothing wrong with aiming for the middle of the road.

I think I mumble a horrified, "Thank you for your time, Sir," before I meander out of his office, utterly and completely crushed.

13

MASTERPIECE OUT OF A MESS

*A*fter our coffee date with Lisa, in which she gushed excitedly about her dates with Marcus, all I want to do is be alone.

I dump my box of ruined cupcakes on the counter because the rectangular box won't fit into the kitchen's garbage can. Then I race up to my bedroom. It's two o'clock in the afternoon, which is good a time as any for a pity party disguised as a nap. I'm so embarrassed. I'm grateful to have smiled my way through girl time believably enough so that I didn't have to dissect and relive the horror that was that awful meeting.

I am smack in the middle of hating myself when a knock interrupts my self-loathing. "Honey cake, I'm coming in."

I draw my comforter up over my head like a true adult,

so Aunt Winnie doesn't have to look upon the face of her loser niece.

She sets something on my nightstand and then sits daintily on the side of my bed, reaching out and resting her hand on my ankle over the blanket. "Fisher called. Said perhaps you might need a friend right now. He's sending over pasta carbonara tonight for dinner for the two of us."

I groan, doubly embarrassed that Fisher knows of my epic failure. "Lenny told Fisher? That's not cool. I want to forget the whole thing ever happened. Now Fisher knows what a joke I am."

Winifred pauses to digest my words before she spits them out. "You are not a joke. Fisher doesn't think anything of the sort. No one does." She rubs my ankle. "Why don't you tell me what happened?"

"Your sister gave birth to a woman, who then gave birth to a loser. That's what happened."

Of all things, Aunt Winifred chuckles. "Is that so? My, my. I'll have to make a note of the blight on our family tree." She peels back the comforter to reveal my reddened face. "Talk to me."

"You don't want to hear it. I tried something big, and it flopped."

"I'll be the judge of that. Walk me through it."

Because Winifred is too stubborn to let me wallow on my own, I spill the story to her, highlighting the worst moments so she understands that I am not leaving this bed for the foreseeable future.

When I finish, Winifred's hand is over her chest. "I can't believe you did that!"

"I know! Such a disaster. I don't know what I was thinking."

Winifred waves off my angst. "Not the mess. You fought for your business with no one prodding you forward. You saw a path you wanted to go down and you marched through the door boldly. That's half the battle, and you conquered it with class. And with no army behind you, either. I thought you said you were a loser. Losers don't do that. They're too afraid to try."

"Don't try to make me feel better. It was a failure. The cupcakes are ruined and so are my chances at baking for The Snuggle Inn."

Winifred stands, ripping my comforter off the bed so I have no choice but to get up. "Come with me. I want you to see something. And bring the tea I set on your nightstand. You don't want to drink tepid tea. That would be the real low moment of the day."

The urge to cling to the mattress is tempting, but I know I can't be a child about this much longer. I have to face the smashed box of cupcakes and deal with the fact that I let myself down today.

I follow Winifred down the steps, my shoulders slumped and my spirit completely dejected. When we reach the kitchen, she pops open the top of the box that should have been thrown away in the outside trash.

I flinch at the massacre, but Winifred directs the turn of my head toward the mess. "Tell me what you see."

"Failure." There is little in me that is willing to sugar-coat the obvious. "Reaching for something I can't handle."

Winifred takes a fork out of the drawer to her right and dips it into the mangled desserts. She pops the bite in her mouth, her eyes closing at the mingled flavors. "Chocolate, vanilla, coffee and something else. Some seasoning."

"Cardamom," I reply glumly, resting my elbows on the table.

Winifred feeds me a bite of the concoction, which I'll admit, doesn't taste bad at all. "It's a good combination, isn't it. I've had each one of your cupcakes on its own, but mixed together like this, it's something entirely new."

I am not in the mood to be cheered up. "Yep. A new mess."

Winifred sets down her fork and pats my arm, giving my wrist a light squeeze. "If the only thing you learn in all of this is that you shouldn't have tried something bold, then you'll have missed the lesson entirely. You've got genius in here," she says, tapping my forehead, "and genius in here," she adds, touching the top of the box. "The Snuggle Inn was never the goal."

"It wasn't? Because I kind of made those cupcakes especially for that job."

Winifred shakes her head, her silver curls barely

moving from their pinned position at the base of her neck. "The goal was to challenge yourself. To take your business to the next level. If The Snuggle Inn isn't the next level, then we'll figure out what is. It's not a defeat, Charlotte; it's a change of direction, is all."

I mull over her words, pondering the wisdom in them. Maybe she's right. I wanted a gig at a restaurant because that seems like the next logical step in expanding my business. What I wanted was to push myself to the next level—to take a leap and land somewhere higher. If it's not The Snuggle Inn, then maybe it's somewhere else.

Winifred pushes the box closer to me. "Spend some time with your bravery, Charlotte. Just because there isn't an immediate reward doesn't mean it wasn't worth the effort. Sometimes it just means that the reward is right in front of you, but it looks different than you thought it would." She moves to the fridge to pull out fixings for a sandwich. "You're not leaving this kitchen until you tell me how you succeeded today. Failure is nothing to be afraid of. Oftentimes it's just another word for success."

My mouth pulls to the side as I contemplate the puzzle she presents to me. Could she be onto something? Could I have done the right thing and landed somewhere better by pushing myself this morning, even though the intended results never came about?

I stare into the box, this time with a more scrutinizing eye. I'm not flinching at the mess, but more intrigued by the mingling of colors and flavors. Winifred was right; the different crumbs mixed together was a nice surprise.

I stand and grab a spatula and two bowls, separating the icing into one and the cakes into the other. I didn't make any peppermint cupcakes for my audition, so the double fudge flavor, the cardamom vanilla bean and the vanilla latte cupcakes actually mix together quite nicely. While I have no desire to make a cupcake out of that mixture, I know there is a way to make something new with the destroyed ingredients.

I grab up a piece of paper, jotting down a few ingredients I will need if I am going to stick to Winifred's assignment and salvage this failure, relabeling it as a victory.

Winifred watches me out of the corner of her eye, a small smile playing on her lips. "Are you still a loser? Or have you found a way to expand your business already?"

I gnaw on my lower lip, formulating a plan that goes beyond this one batch of ruined cupcakes. "I don't know yet, but if I don't try, I'll never find out."

Aunt Winifred raises her teacup to me. "That's the spirit, Charlotte the Brave."

For the first time today, I actually believe her label for me might be the right one after all.

14

GOING TO WAR

*M*arianne balks at the display. "These are the cutest things I've ever seen. Please don't let me try to make them. They look complicated."

Marianne is right that the tiny swirls require a little more dexterity than frosting a cupcake. "Deal. They started out as the crumbs of a dozen ruined cupcakes, but I think they turned out alright. Maybe even better than the original design."

Winifred beams while Karen and Agnes gape at the foam block with the sucker sticks jutting out from the top.

"They're adorable. Too pretty to eat," Agnes remarks, turning the block this way and that so she can view the cake pops from all angles.

Karen covers her mouth with her hand. "We get to eat those? I thought they were just decorations."

"I dropped a box of cupcakes yesterday, and Winifred

challenged me to turn my failure into a win. So I spent some time with the ingredients and realized that the three basic flavors I offer every month actually taste really nice together. Cake pops aren't all that complicated; they just take a bit of time and patience. But it might be the perfect product for my business, because all it takes is a few smashed cupcakes that either got dropped or didn't rise properly, and a bit of frosting to wet the crumbs so they can be formed into a ball." I pick up a half-used bag of green chocolate wafer melts. "Then I put it on a sucker stick and dipped it in melted chocolate. The rest is just details."

Agnes motions for me to pass her the grocery list pad off the refrigerator. "Toy stores. You need to sell these at toy stores. Or anywhere that caters to children."

I purse my lips. "I was just thinking of putting them on my website for people to order along with the regular cupcakes."

Agnes shakes her head. "No, no. We're going aggressive with these. I'm sure they're normal for big city folk, but they're going to blow people's minds in this town. If they taste good, you've got a smash hit, my dear."

I frown at Agnes. "Of course they taste good. I don't pride myself on things that look pretty but taste like sand. Try them."

Karen shakes her head. "Oh, no. They're too beautiful. I'm afraid to bite into it. It would ruin the design."

I chuckle at the reason for Karen's hesitation. "Seriously, I made them for us to try."

Agnes takes the first one off the foam block. "If they taste even a little palatable, they'll sell like hotcakes. Charlotte, these are adorable."

I bob on the balls of my feet, glowing with the warmth from their words. I can't believe how simple a switch it was from cupcakes to cake pops. I have the key ingredients on hand already. It's the next logical step for my business. Selling them in toy stores? I'll admit, that thought never occurred to me, but I am not opposed to trying that angle. I'm happy I took Winifred's advice, refusing to let the label of failure remain permanent.

Marianne doesn't hold back. When she takes the first bite, her eyes roll with delirium. "Are you kidding me? You've known how to make these this entire time, and I'm only just now tasting this? You've been holding out on me. This is incredible! I can taste each flavor. So good together!"

Karen casts me a look laced with mild worry. "Are you sure I should eat it? It's so pretty."

Marianne answers for me with a vigorous nod. "Your mind is about to be blown, Karen."

I love watching people take the first bite of my creations. The closing of the eyes, the "mm" noise, the inhale followed by the contented exhale.

Never gets old.

The fact that this moment was made possible because

of a crushing defeat is just about the best feeling in the world.

Agnes munches on her cake pop while she jots down a list of places she thinks we could sell this new item. "The overhead wouldn't change much, but the time involved in making these is something to consider."

She is not wrong, though it's nothing too arduous that I couldn't work this into the weekly rotation of things I create in the kitchen.

"Can you do different designs?" Agnes asks, tapping the tip of her pen on the table.

"Sure. Balloons, emoji faces, cats. The easiest are the abstract swirls and whatnot, but the other designs aren't all that difficult. So long as the shape is round, the sky is the limit."

Winifred takes the empty chair at the table, since I have no interest in sitting. I am too amped up from the victory to slow down enough to sit. "Cats and dogs?" Winifred inquires.

I do my best to conjure up a decent image of what I am capable of. "Sure."

Winifred points to Agnes' list. "Add the pet shop, Agnes."

"They're not pet friendly," I point out.

"Not for the pets, for the pet owners. We're not ruling anything out."

Marianne sings a cheery, "No bad ideas in brainstorming!"

The list grows in time with my heart swelling. I did it. I turned a failure into a victory.

"What's that smile for, honey cake?" Winifred inquires.

"Oh, nothing. I'm glad I didn't give up. I sure am grateful for you girls."

"How much does a dozen cost to make?" Agnes asks me, her eyes on the paper.

I rattle off a number, amazed at how inexpensive these were to create.

Agnes jots down a few more things and then holds up the list. "I'd bake a few dozen more of these cake pops, Charlotte. Starting tomorrow morning, I'm taking samples to the businesses on Peach Street. Marianne, can you type up a proposal using these numbers? I'd like to have something to hand out that has all the information they'll need for ordering."

My eyes widen as Marianne snatches at the sheet without pause. "Of course! I can do that on Charlotte's computer right now."

The gusto with which these women support each other (and me) is always surprising, no matter how often it happens. All I did was come up with a new product to add to my business, and they are ready to go to war for me, peddling my cake pops far and wide.

"You don't have to do that," I tell the ladies. "I can just put them up on the website."

Karen takes her first bite, her eyes closing and then widening. "I was expecting it to be pretty and that's all, but these flavors are incredible. Charlotte, this is amazing. Agnes, I'll take Pear Street and pass out flyers." She starts counting on her fingers. "There are eight business on Pear Street, and I'll need probably two cake pops per business. A variety of designs so they can see what a great addition these would be to their checkout area."

Winifred nods. "It's the perfect impulse purchase."

Marianne races up to my bedroom to pull out my laptop and start typing up the information.

I swear, these women could rule the world.

Luckily, they are taking me along for the ride while I learn that there is far more to my business—and myself—than I ever imagined.

CAKE POPS AND ICE CREAM

*I*t would be pretty shady of me to send Marianne and the Live Forever Club out to pitch my cake pops to local business owners without hitting the pavement myself. Though, given my track record of securing jobs at businesses, I'm not sure I am the best person to try this out.

Still, I head down Main Street, taking the left side of the street while Winifred covers the right. I am grateful my first stop is the Nosy Newsy. Frank isn't all that intimidating.

"Hey, new girl. The flowers aren't particularly chatty today." Frank grins at me, showing off the fact that he is missing one of his teeth.

I smile at him and tug out an envelope from my pocket, hiding it in the daisies for Logan to find later. "That's okay. I'll give them something to talk about. A note for the flowers and a letter for you." I hand him the sheet with my prices listed on it, along with photos of different designs I can do so businesses can order whichever cake pops best suit each individual business.

Frank looks the page over appraisingly, then glances at me. "What's all this about? I thought you were a one-trick pony. Cupcakes and nothing else."

"Cake pops aren't all that big a leap, but they're super cute and they travel as well as a lollipop. My own designs, my own flavors. I'm stopping at all the businesses on the street to see if any would like to carry my cake pops at their stores."

Frank narrows one eye at me. "You thought a newsstand would be a good place for baked goods?" But even though the skepticism is thick in his tone, as he says it, I can see genuine consideration on his face. "I mean, it's not the worst idea. I do sell candy. It's not a far leap from a candy bar, and a heck of a lot classier. But this is a roadside business, if you haven't noticed. I can't have things that dust might settle on and ruin."

I show him the cake pops, pointing out the clear wrappers shielding the vulnerable area. "Already thought of that."

"I see you have. Hmm. It says here you do different designs. Could you do something specific to my store? I don't know what, but if I buy a few to sell, I don't want something they could pick up at the store down the street. It would need to be something they could only get here."

My mouth pulls to the side. "An exclusive design is a good idea. Any suggestions?"

"Can you do a miniature newsstand?"

I grimace. "I don't think so. It needs to be round or roundish."

Frank hands the slip back to me. "Give it some thought because I'm not opposed to trying it out. I'm all about supporting local businesses."

I chew on my lower lip as I hand him a cake pop to try, so at least he has a reference for the flavor.

"That's real good, Charlotte. Almost too pretty to eat, but somehow I'll manage." He winks and chuckles as he finishes the cake pop. "Oh, yeah. I could sell those. But the design needs to be unique to my store, otherwise no dice."

"Fair point. Give me the weekend to think about it and I'll get back to you."

When a woman's voice sounds from behind me, I grimace at being caught at the Nosy Newsy, even though I know I've done nothing wrong. "Well, if it isn't Charlotte sniffing around the newsstand again. If I had a nickel for all the times I found you here, chatting up Frank, I would be quite the wealthy woman."

I turn, donning a friendly smile because, despite Delia's imagined feud with me, I have no beef with her. "Hey, Delia. Good to see you. I was pitching Frank my new business idea. Want to try it?"

Delia studies the tray in my gloved hands. Though this is hardly the weather to be going door to door, it seems that is the most effective way to pass out proposals and pretty desserts. "Those are edible?" Her frustration with me melts away when I hand her a yellow cake pop with a smiley face design on the front. "That is the cutest thing!" she takes a bite and groans in satisfaction. "Oh, that's not just a sugary taste, either. It's got some real depth to it."

Frank watches Delia enjoy the treat with unedited infatuation. I love the way he stares at her. Even though Delia is occasionally sour towards me because she assumes I am sniffing around her man, I like seeing something good happen for her.

"You like it, Delia?" Franks asks her.

"I love it." She points to the stick. "Are these going to be available for order on your website?"

I shake my head. "You can only buy them at Sweetwater Falls businesses. I was thinking of selling them at the Nosy Newsy too, but they need to be designed specifically for Frank's business. Any ideas?"

Delia's mouth pulls to the side while she chews. "I'll give it some thought. These are delicious, Charlotte. Truly. I haven't had a dessert this good since your last cupcake. Before you, all we were stuck with was crappy pie from Bill's Diner and the occasional scoop of ice cream." She sucks the chocolate off the stick. "Which, incidentally, I had after Nick and Nancy's party went belly up. I took one of your cupcakes for the road, Charlotte. After seeing Tom like that," she pauses to shiver, "I needed as much distraction in the form of sugar that I could get. One cupcake wasn't enough."

"Understandable."

"I can't believe there weren't more people eating out, drowning their sorrows in the same way. It was only me and Marcus for the longest time. And let me tell you, he is boring. Nice enough, but not a stellar conversationalist. I had to carry most of the interaction."

I'll bet that was a real struggle.

My brows furrow together. "Wait, you went out for ice cream the night of Nick and Nancy's party?"

Delia nods. "After the police started to dismiss us, I went to The Snuggle Inn for some ice cream. Well, I went in because I wanted a good dinner, but I opted for dessert instead. Sometimes you just need what you need. Marcus was eating by himself, too, so we got to chatting." Her eyes light up, and I can tell she has fresh gossip on the tip of her tongue. "Speaking of needing what you need, did you hear about Lisa Swanson? Single only a few months and already out on a date. I heard that she was out with Marcus two days ago!"

My head bobs. "After all she's been through this year, I don't think anyone would begrudge her a little joy. If Marcus makes her smile, so much the better. She deserves as many happy moments as she can get. They've been in short supply up until he started taking her out those few times."

Delia grips my elbow. "Have they been out more than once?"

I shouldn't have said that, though there's nothing I can do about the slip now. "Lisa's happy, Delia. Let's not make a big production about it, otherwise she might feel self-conscious."

Delia's brows raise. "Well, she should. He's at least fifteen years younger than she is."

I really don't want to be having this conversation, so I steer her back to the information I need. "You said you and Marcus were the only two people eating at The Snuggle Inn for a while that night. You're sure it was the night of Nick and Nancy's party?"

Delia shoots me a wry look. "Kinda hard to forget something like that. Yes, as soon as the police cleared me, I went straight there. Smelling that ham cooking all that time was torture. I was starving."

I take a step back, mulling over her words as I cast Frank a wan smile. "Thanks for your time, Frank. I'll do some thinking about a design for the Nosy Newsy and get back to you."

Frank bobs his head, though his attention is wholly on Delia. "Sounds good."

I spin on my heel, my mind wrapping itself around the new fact Delia just laid in my lap.

Marcus wasn't at home all night with his golden retriever. He was at The Snuggle Inn.

Why would he lie about that? Why would he say he

was home all night when he was clearly out of the house the evening that Tom was discovered to be murdered?

I don't know what this means, other than that there is more to Marcus' story than he wanted me to know.

Before Lisa falls harder for Marcus, I need to get to the bottom of this and figure out just how much I need to worry about Lisa spending more time with Marcus. The last thing she needs is to fall for a murderer hiding in plain sight.

16

INTERROGATING MARCUS

*M*eeting up with Lisa Swanson just before her date with Marcus isn't the best way to plan an interrogation, but it'll have to do, since I have no way to organically bump into Marcus.

The place they've decided to meet up at is a soup nook I haven't been to before. Though any place called The Soup Alleyoop deserves a visit.

I'm not sure what I was expecting from the name, but it certainly fits the atmosphere. The menu is entirely soup and beverages, and on the walls are arcade basketball games. It's actually a cute idea for a restaurant. The floor is honey-colored hardwood with red markings for a free-throw line in front of each hoop.

Lisa is more than happy to let me horn in on her time, not even sighing when I pull out my sheet cataloging the addition to my business. "Each store who orders from me should have their own design, don't you think? Otherwise it's just a silly chain store item you could get anywhere. But this way, you can only buy the marbled bouncy ball looking cake pops at the Toy Chest. You can only buy the cat cake pops at the pet store."

"I love that. Because you're right, it makes the cake pops you find there special, instead of something you could get anywhere." She scours the sheet for flaws, which is what I was hoping she would do. "It looks solid, Charlotte. Seriously, this is a great idea."

I beam at the praise. "None of it would be happening if it weren't for you. You're the one who helped me turn my dream into an actual business a few months ago."

"All I did was put your passion on a piece of paper." Lisa is easy to talk to, especially when I ask her about the new gym she's been going to. Though I know I should excuse myself before Marcus arrives for their date, I draw out the conversation, asking detailed questions about her workouts so that when noon rolls around, I can make small talk with Marcus before I leave them to their date.

When Marcus finally arrives, I stand up and shake his hand, looking like I am greeting him at an interview. "Hi, Marcus. I was just keeping Lisa company for a bit. How are you?"

"Can't complain."

I should find a better way to work my borderline accusation into polite conversation, but after a few sentences, I want to get to the bottom of things and get out of here. "I've been working on some new desserts. Delia said she saw you the night of Nick and Nancy's party at The Snuggle Inn. Do you think I should try my hand at making and selling ice cream?"

Not exactly smooth, but it's direct enough without being overtly accusatory (I hope).

The point is made because Marcus' eyes widen at being caught. "Oh, yeah. I guess I was out that night. Just getting some food and heading back to my house. Like I said before, it was a quiet night. I didn't try their ice cream. I don't have much of a sweet tooth, so my opinion isn't the one you should go by."

I tilt my head to the side, feigning innocence in my curiosity. "Why didn't you go to the party? The ham smelled amazing." I shove my hands in my pockets. "Not that you would have enjoyed any of it, though, being that the murder cut the party short."

Marcus sits down with a dejected huff. "Look, I'm not one to talk bad about people. I'm sure Nick and Nancy had a good reason for doing what they did to Tom, but when he told me about it, I didn't want any part of their Christmas party. So yeah, I got dinner at The Snuggle Inn, but other than that, I stayed home, even though I had RSVP'd to the party two weeks earlier."

I reclaim my seat while Lisa pats his hand. "What happened, Marcus?" she asks.

I'm grateful I don't have to dig for the answers. It's nice to have a little help this time.

Marcus shoves his fists into his jacket pockets. "Tom and I used to walk our dogs together a few times a month. He mentioned that his dog, Beanie, got loose and ran into their yard. They took him into their house while they waited for Tom to come pick up Beanie. Apparently, Beanie peed on Nancy's rug while they were waiting for Tom. Nancy threw a big fit, even after Tom offered to pay to have it professionally cleaned. Apparently, that wasn't good enough. Beanie sniffed this. He slobbered on that. On and on until she guilted him into paying for a cleaning service to come out and shine up their entire house. Cost Tom a couple hundred dollars."

I whistle, floored at the gall Nancy has when she gets bent out of shape about something. "That's intense."

"That's the right word for it. Well, Tom thought that was that, so he put it out of his mind. Well, last week, he got a bill for a second cleaning done at Nick and Nancy's house. I guess Nancy hired the company to come out and clean again and told them to keep billing Tom. She said the company missed a few spots on the first cleaning." Marcus shakes his head. "After that, I didn't really feel too jolly, so I opted not to go to the party. Forgot that I broke up my night alone with dinner at The Snuggle Inn, though. That was a long night. Have you heard Delia talk when she's worked up? Her words per minute rate is astounding."

My stomach sinks that perhaps the person I need to be

interrogating is not the man sitting across from me, but rather Mrs. Claus herself.

I kiss Lisa atop her head and thank Marcus for letting me barge in on the beginning of their date. Before I leave, I stop at the counter to pay for two drinks to be sent over to them. Hopefully that will get more conversation going between them that has nothing to do with a murder or Nancy, who is turning out to be the sneakiest woman I have ever met.

17

LOUSY DATE

I like going out with Logan, though usually our time together isn't weighted by this much talk of murder. "Are you sure Marcus said Nancy tried to force Tom to pay to have her house cleaned twice?"

My head bobs as I chew on the end of my straw. The movie we saw tonight wasn't bad, but we were both too distracted for anything other than an intense action film to hold our attention. A foreign film complete with subtitles left too much space for my brain to mull over the facts of the case as I know them.

Apparently, Logan had the same issue.

"That's what Marcus said. After the way Nancy handled the bounced check she gave me, I believe him. She does not like to pay for things."

Logan's fingers lace through mine. "I'm sorry. I'm being a terrible date. I can't get the case off my mind, even though I'm off the clock. This was supposed to be a fun date, and I'm being boring."

"I hardly think talking about murder is boring. But it's not exactly a night off the clock for you if you're still thinking as if you're on the job."

"True enough."

I swing our joined hands back and forth while we walk down the lamplit street. It's too cold for a walk, but neither of us have the patience to sit still at a restaurant right now. "If you're looking for a change of topics, I've got one for you."

"Please. I beg of you. Distract me so I don't show you how completely obsessive I can be and turn you off for good."

I cast him a withering look. "Like that's possible." I give his hand a squeeze. "The Live Forever Club does a Christmas dinner every year together on Christmas Eve. Just them, plus Marianne, and now me." I keep my eyes from him as I figure out on the fly how to phrase my question. "I spent last Christmas alone in my apartment. Growing up, my parents never made a big deal about Christmas, either. But this year, I'm with Winifred, and she's into the friends-as-family kind of thing. Maybe it's too soon, but if you don't have plans Christmas Eve, maybe you would want to come to Winifred's dinner?" My neck shrinks as my cheeks heat. That was definitely too forward. "What am I saying? Of course you have plans. It's Christmas Eve! Sorry I asked. We've only been dating a couple of months. I'm getting ahead of myself. Forget I mention it."

Logan stops our stroll and turns to face me, his expression stern. "Why did you do that? Invite me and then sabotage the offer?"

I can't look up at him. Who knew that he would look like a ski model in his fur-lined jacket? "I dunno. I realized how big a deal it was after I said it. Inviting you to holiday family things is probably something for couples who have been together for a year or two, not dating only a few months." I reach out and tap the toe of my shoe to his. "I don't want to scare you away."

Logan cups my chin and tilts my head up. Instead of a response, he touches his lips to mine. It's a whisper of a kiss, but I hold onto it because it's a gift from a man I not only like, but respect as a good and capable person.

His words fan across my nose. "I'm not scared of being close to you, Miss Charlotte. In fact, there's nothing I want more."

I blink at him, stunned that even through my ineptitude, I still managed not to scare him away.

He turns back to the sidewalk and tucks my arm in the crook of his elbow, where it belongs. I love that he likes me in his space. "Christmas Eve family dinner at your place. It's a date."

My insides warm. "Aunt Winnie is making a big ham. It'll be a good day."

"Will you be there?"

"Of course."

"Then I'm sure it will be a great day."

We walk in companionable silence before I get the sneaking suspicion that Logan's mind is back on his job. "You solving a murder in your mind?" I ask, bumping my hip to his.

Logan cuts me a sidelong glance. "Trying to. Was I that obvious?"

"No, you're just that good at your job. Come on. Out loud with it."

Logan expels a heavy sigh. "I can't shake the fact that Nancy and Nick have kept things from us at every turn. None of the things are even all that damning, but it begs the question of why. Why would they need to keep from the police that they hired Helen? Honestly, I could have crossed their name off the list of suspects a long time ago if we didn't keep turning up more lies they've been feeding us."

"Have there been more? Helen, sure. What else?"

"The neighbors saw a car they didn't recognize in the driveway at four-thirty the day of the party, but Nick and Nancy swear they were alone in the house at that time. The first guest arrived ten minutes after that, according to Nancy."

"Weird."

"The neighbor gave me the vaguest description of the car: a blue sedan. So, not Helen's car, and not one belonging to Nick and Nancy, and not one belonging to anyone on the guest list for the party. So now I have a mystery car I have to deal with."

"Any ideas?"

"Not really. I mean, it's barely a lead, and when I dig to the bottom and find who was driving the blue sedan, will that be another useless piece of the puzzle? It's so much effort to get each bit of truth. I can't tell which parts are important to solving Tom's murder and which aren't."

My mouth pulls to the side. "That sounds like quite the headache." I keep close to his side, leeching out whatever unhappiness might surface. "Maybe the blue sedan belongs to the housekeeper."

"Could be, but according to Nick and Nancy, the house-keeper wasn't there that day."

My shoulders fall. "Oh, right. Nick told me he and Nancy cleaned the house the day of the party because the housekeeper wasn't available."

Logan nods. "Another headache is that my dad's all upset because Tom doesn't have any family, so there isn't going to be a funeral. I told him I would help him orga-nize one, but he wasn't interested in that. He's grieving on top of working overtime, which is a bad combina-tion." When the wind picks up, Logan switches sides with me so he can bear the brunt of the breeze. "I know this will surprise you, but my dad can get surly sometimes."

"I am shocked to hear that," I deadpan.

Something pings in my brain. "Logan, there was a blue

sedan parked in the driveway when I was bringing my desserts to their house. It's why I had to park on the street."

Logan's steps slow. "I didn't realize. You didn't happen to see any distinguishing features, like, oh, say, a license plate?"

I stop walking and close my eyes, trying my best to picture any detail that might be telling about the car. Of course the license plate escapes me. I had no reason to catalog that particular detail. "The back window was cracked. The person was coming out of the side of the house when we got there. They got in the car and left, but I didn't want to park in the driveway in their spot because I didn't want to get blocked in if someone else pulled in behind me."

"Any description of the person? Man? Woman?"

"It was evening. Too shadowy. This is going to bother me. Hold on." I take out my phone and call Marianne. "Hey, girl. Real quick."

"You're calling me on your date? Tell Logan well done." Her sarcasm makes me laugh.

"I couldn't live without your voice for three whole hours."

Marianne starts singing off-key just to make me smile. "What can I do for you?"

"The night of the Christmas party," I pause for Marianne's groan, "when we were bringing our desserts in, I had to park in the street because there was a blue sedan in the driveway. Do you remember that?"

"I remember. The back window had a crack. I can't imagine how cold the interior must have been for the drive home."

"I saw a person coming out of the house and getting into the car before it pulled out of the driveway. Any chance you saw who it was?"

Marianne pauses. "I didn't get a good look. But you're right, they pulled out as we were getting the cupcakes out of the trunk."

"Thanks. That's all I needed to know."

"Glad I could be helpful. Tell Logan he's a lousy date if the two of you are talking about an unsolved murder on your night out."

"Hey!" Logan protests, having overheard her jab.

"I'll be sure to tell him exactly that." I end the call, chewing on my lower lip as I factor in this bit of information. "I'm guessing your murderer drives a blue sedan, Logan. That, or it's another dead end."

Logan tugs out his phone and relays the information to his father. "I'll take it. Thanks. I needed one thing to make sense in all of this."

"Really? That seems like I made it more confusing for you."

"I needed some direction, which you gave me."

Though I wish I could solve this entire thing for him, I am grateful to have been helpful in pushing him toward the next clue, whatever that may be.

Logan faces me, holding my hands and swinging them

between us. "Marianne was right; I am being a lousy date. Let me make it up to you? There's a neighborhood nearby that goes all out with Christmas decorations. It's impressive, and a great way to erase the work stink in the air and replace it with something jolly."

"That sounds like just the ticket. Lead the way."

And just like that, our time together turns from murder to candy canes, which is the mark of a truly good date.

ROCK CANDY

I always hope that my business goes well, but I honestly did not expect the cake pops would be this popular. What used to be a day of baking to fill the orders for that half of the week is now two days of baking, frosting, rolling and dipping things into melted chocolate. It's a good problem to have because the Live Forever Club made sure that I priced myself sustainably, so the business' bank account isn't suffering one bit.

I have nothing I am saving up for, other than a place of my own to sell my goods. That goal is a long way off, but that doesn't crush my spirits at all.

I whisk egg whites while the kitchen fills itself with the smell of chocolate, peppermint and cardamom.

I love the look of the crushed candy canes sprinkled on the top of the peppermint frosting. The hot cocoa cupcakes add a dash of happiness to the kitchen as every surface is taken over by baked goods.

I do need to find a kitchen to bake in, even if a storefront is a long way off. Aunt Winifred never acts bothered that I have basically commandeered an essential portion of her home for most of the week now, but it can't carry on like this for much longer.

By the morning when my deliveries are scheduled, I am beat, and the kitchen is completely taken over without a speck of bare counter in sight. Even though all the cupcakes are boxed, and the cake pops are packaged properly and ready for pickup, there isn't a place for Winifred to sit and enjoy her breakfast. She doesn't complain one bit when I set up a TV tray and bring her coddled eggs and fruit so she can eat in the living room, but I feel like rubbish for crowding my great-aunt out of her own kitchen.

When my customers start to arrive, I happily hand out their orders, grateful that I am starting to see smidgens of counter space again. My hair is in a nice bun atop my head and I am even wearing the bracelet that Jeanette gave me earlier this month. Though I have spots of flour on my clothes, the bracelet makes me feel stepped up. It's supposed to infuse me with serenity, so I claim that slice of peace for myself and wear it proudly on my wrist to fend off any anxiety that might come my way.

I have no idea if stuff like that actually works, but it's pretty, so I pretend it does.

I am happy to see friendly and familiar faces. Each time I recognize a person, it makes me feel like I belong here, like I am part of this perfect town.

"Good morning, Marcus. I've got your order of a dozen assorted right here. Repeat customers are my favorite."

Marcus smiles at me. "Thank goodness you do this. It makes me look like I'm a competent host, putting out fancy desserts like these. Hopefully you do this forever, because the bar is set pretty high now for my movie nights."

"Absolutely. Let me know what your guests think of the peppermint cupcakes. Those are the flavor of the month."

"Will do." He inhales with a smile as his eyelashes flutter. "I love the smell of this kitchen. If only each order came with this scent. Then I could travel with it all day. Though, I'm not sure my dog would appreciate the chocolate smell. He's got a playdate today."

"That's nice. Anyone local?"

"Beanie."

I tilt my head to the side. "Tom's dog?"

"Not Tom's anymore. Lisa decided to step in and adopt Beanie, so he wouldn't have to go live at the pound. She's got a good heart."

I cannot picture Lisa with a dog. She is well-manicured and organized in a way that gives me the impression that perhaps a dog might not be welcome if he has the propensity to get in the way of her plans for the day. I can't wait to see how that works out. "Lisa does have a good heart. I'll have to stop by and visit her this week to see how Beanie is acclimating."

And to see if Lisa has lost her mind.

"Delia was thrilled. She hates that dog. She even offered to buy Beanie a dog crate so Lisa could transport him to her place."

"I remember Delia mentioning that Beanie is a bit loud in the morning." Not sure how Lisa is going to take to that, but more power to her.

Marcus leans in conspiratorially. "When we went into Delia's house to get the crate, you'll never guess what I found."

"What?"

"About a dozen nutcrackers."

"Huh. I guess this town has a thing for them. Nick and Nancy have a huge collection."

Marcus shakes his head at me. "They were all Nick and Nancy's."

My mouth pulls to the side. "How can you be sure?"

"She bragged about it to us. Said she steals a couple every year as her souvenir. It's a game she plays with herself." He shrugs. "Whatever makes you happy, I guess. Petty thievery isn't my bag, so I don't get the appeal."

"Living on the edge, I guess."

I know that Karen shoplifts on occasion to make herself feel young, but then she leaves the money for her purchases in the penny jar by the checkout. So she isn't actually stealing anything, but she still gets that thrill of doing something scandalous.

Marcus balances the cupcake box in one hand while holding his water bottle in the other. "I told Delia she has to return the gold one. It's worth a couple hundred dollars." He rolls his eyes. "I have no idea what makes a nutcracker worth more than thirty bucks, but I'm not an avid collector. Nick likes to talk about his collectibles, so I know he'll be wanting that one back."

Dread paints my features. "Oh, no. It's worth three hundred dollars. Nancy accused me of stealing it. She very much wants that thing back."

Marcus sighs. "That's not cool. Nancy really accused you of stealing it?"

I nod, wishing Delia's petty crime hadn't blown back on me.

When the doorbell rings, I smile at the face on the other side of the glass door, motioning for her to come inside. "Hi, Jeanette. Good to see you."

"I came to pick up my order of cake pops." She stops short, her long skirt swooshing as she fans her face. "Oh, you're wearing the bracelet I gave you! That makes me happy."

I display the jewelry proudly. "It's given me serenity to keep me going this morning, so the gemstones are holding up nicely."

"That's wonderful, Charlotte." She glances around with wide eyes, taking in the tall stacks of boxes all over.

"Wow. I had no idea you did so much business. Charlotte, you've outgrown your space already."

I grimace at the truth in her statement. "Unfortunately, that seems to be the case. I'm going to need to start looking into renting kitchen space soon. Aunt Winnie is wonderful to let me bake everything here, but at some point, I'm sure she would like to actually be able to use her kitchen."

Marcus points to my wrist. "You made that, Jeanette?"

Jeanette fluffs her waist length red hair. "I sure did."

"And you sell them at Sweetwater Fountains? I haven't been in there in a while."

"I do sell them. Are you interested in picking one up for yourself?"

He shakes his head. "I want to get Lisa something special for Christmas but not too special that I freak her out." He points to the bracelet. "That looks the right amount of special."

"Stop by later today and I'll show you my selection."

"It's a plan." He holds up his cupcake box. "Thanks, Charlotte. I'll see you later."

Jeanette leans her hip against the fridge after Marcus exits, crossing her arms over her chest instead of taking her delivery and leaving. "You don't want a storefront?" she inquires, jerking her chin toward the delivery boxes. "Because it looks like you could use one of those that has a kitchen in the back."

"That's the dream, but it's a big expense. I'm still a new business, so risks like that aren't fiscally responsible yet."

Marianne would be so proud that I used the words "fiscally responsible" without her prompting.

"So your bridge step would be renting kitchen space, which would be significantly less expensive than a full-on storefront. Then once you have enough saved up there, you'd want your own place."

"You say it all like it's a simple leap, but I don't know of anything like that around here. And I need this to be a Sweetwater Falls business."

"Need?" Jeanette tilts her head to the side.

"I can't fathom setting up a business even a mile outside the city limits. I love this town. It's the first place where I've felt like I belong. These people took a chance on me, buying my cupcakes when they barely knew me. My business is only going well because of them. It would be a slap in the face to the town I love if I opened up outside the city limits, though I'm sure Hamshire has more options."

A small smile plays at the corner of Jeanette's lips. "I felt the same way when I opened up my business." Her bangled wrist motions to the orders piled up all around us. "How much can you swing to rent a kitchen, so you can spread your wings a little and expand your orders?"

I rattle off a meager number, wondering why Jeanette is asking for specifics.

"That'll work." She plucks up her box and moves to exit, tossing a few words over her shoulder. "Stop by

Sweetwater Fountains after you send off your last order. I might have an idea of a kitchen that has space for you."

My heart nearly stops in my chest. "What? Are you serious?"

"Serious and sure that you can't keep on like you are." She pops open the top of her box, gasping at my hard work. "What did you do? These aren't the designs you had on the sheet."

Insecurity rattles my bones. "If you don't like them, I can send you with some emoji smiley faces instead. I thought each business should have its own cake pop design, so people can only get a certain kind at your business. Give them one more reason to come into the shop."

I don't expect Jeannette to pull one out to gape at it, but I am grateful when I see a glimmer of wonder dancing in her eyes. "Charlotte, are these edible crystals?"

"It's rock candy, dyed to match the gemstones you sell in your store. It's a cake with a mirrored glaze over it to match those mirrored balls you have on a few of your fountains. Then rock candy on top. I thought you could try to upsell the matching bracelets with each cake pop that has the edible gemstone in that color."

Jeannette's eyes glisten with unshed emotion. "This is truly spectacular, Charlotte. I can't even begin to tell you how amazing this is. I wasn't thinking about the competition from the other businesses, being that you're selling to everyone. You really made this design just for Sweetwater Fountains?"

I nod solemnly. "You can't even buy them on my website. If they want a Sweetwater Fountains cake pop, they have to go inside your store. Same as the ones I made for Nosy Newsy. Frank's are white with black lettering that read 'Extra! Extra!' I wanted everyone's to be unique to their business. Give people one more reason to shop in Sweetwater Falls."

Jeannette's hand goes over her heart. "I love everything about that and everything about you. Make sure you come by the store today as soon as you're finished up here."

After she leaves, I realize that it might be all day before I am finished up here. Even after the orders are all filled, the kitchen is in desperate need of a wipe down.

Actually, it needs more than that. I take a deep breath and call Nick and Nancy, donning my most chipper tone. "Hi, Nick. Good to hear from you." *And not Nancy.* "Could I get the name and number of your housekeeper? Your place was spotless, and I was thinking of surprising my aunt with a sparklingly clean home to thank her for letting me set up my business in her kitchen."

"Oh, sure. Though, the day of the party, each sparkle and shine was our doing," Nick reminds me with a chuckle. "Tell Emily we recommended her. She gives out client referrals and we could use a discount."

"Will do." I take down the name and number, then call the housekeeper before I can talk myself out of the extra expense. Aunt Winnie deserves her house to be cared for better than I can currently make that happen. I book the cleaning for the next morning, grateful she had an opening.

Emily of Emily's Cleaning Service will get this house back in order, so I can focus on baking and figure out a way to stop trashing my sweet aunt's home.

BURGER JOINT

*T*he windchimes have a calming effect when I walk into Sweetwater Fountains at one in the afternoon with Marianne by my side. After we pay Jeannette a visit, we are going to check out one of Marianne's favorite nature trails because I have never been, and it seems like a nice way to spend an afternoon, even while it's cold out.

Marianne points at the checkout counter. "Oo! I didn't get to see those. Oh, Charlotte. They're gorgeous! So ornate. I couldn't picture the rock candy on the tops of the cake pops. And the mirror glaze? Can you show me how to do that?"

"Of course!" Though, to be fair, that wasn't exactly easy.

I can't help but light up when I see the cake pop

display near the register. But when I get closer, I see only half of them are there.

Did I forget to put in the full two dozen she ordered? I knew something like this would happen. I'm going too fast, trying to get everything accomplished. I didn't bother slowing down to make sure everything was in order.

Jeannette finishes up a sale and then glides over to us, her flowy hippie dress fluttering out behind her. "Charlotte, I've been thinking about you all morning. I'm glad you're here. You came at the perfect time." She motions around her store. "Mid-afternoon lull, as you can see."

I touch my forehead, worry pouring out of me like sweat. "Jeannette, I'm so sorry. Did I only put half the cake pops in your order?"

She glances to the stand, then turns back to me, clapping her hands like a giddy girl. "No, they've been sold!"

My nose scrunches. "A dozen? Already? They've only been out since this morning."

"They're a hit, Charlotte. And you were right; pairing them with a bracelet that has a matching gemstone was a fantastic idea. I've sold more bracelets this morning than I have all week."

My mouth falls open. "Are you serious? That's amazing!"

Jeannette's eyebrows dance as she tugs her long red hair back into her fist. "That's not the only amazing thing. You mentioned this morning that you were outgrowing

Winifred's kitchen and that you were in the market for renting one."

Marianne answers for me. "Oh, yes. We need to start pricing out some options. With the added burden of making the cake pops, it's become problematic to take over Winifred's kitchen full-time."

Jeannette nods. "It's a good problem to have." She motions around her store. "This used to be a burger joint, way, way back in the day. When I moved to Sweetwater Falls, the burger shop had long since closed and the place was on the market." She leans against the wall, eyeing a huge fountain that stands at least six feet high. "I used to live in a big city. Crowded. Smoggy. When I moved here, I felt much like you do, Charlotte. I knew I had finally come home. So I opened up Sweetwater Fountains in the old burger shop."

I glance around at the structure. "You would never guess this used to be a restaurant. You've completely transformed the place. Well done."

"Not completely." She motions for Marianne and me to follow her. She pushes open the door behind the register, leading us into the backroom. "I have no need for a kitchen."

Sure enough, there are hallmarks of a kitchen: a giant grill, two ovens, an industrial refrigerator and plenty of cupboards. But much of the space has been taken over by inventory for Sweetwater Fountains.

"This morning when I asked you how much you'd be

willing to pay to rent a kitchen, you quoted me a little higher than I would charge you for this, if you want it."

I have a hard time computing her words. I blink at her, perplexed that she could say something that sounds exactly like paradise. She can't possibly mean...

"Are you serious?" Marianne squeals, bobbing on the balls of her feet. She confirms the price with Jeannette and then shouts, "Yes! We'll take it! That's well within our budget. Charlotte, do you know what this means?"

I shake my head. "You're cutting me a deal. You need this space for your inventory. I would be in your way."

Jeannette waves off my concern. "What I need is help with the rent. There's another room back here that I can use for storage. I wouldn't say no to some help clearing out my things from the kitchen here, but if you want it and the check clears, the space is yours. All of it. There's even a back entrance behind those boxes there, so you wouldn't have to carry cupcakes through the storefront." She holds up her hands. "It's not your end goal of having your own bakery, but it's a bridge step. It's one leap closer to getting to your dream. And it's a huge leap closer to me not worrying about making rent every single month." She walks further inside, pointing at the appliances. "Everything has been unplugged since I moved in because I don't use it, but I was told it all works. If anything needs updating, that would be on you to do. Upkeep would be on you. But the building stuff is on me."

I cover my mouth with my hands when something that

sounds suspiciously like a sob belts out of me. I'm not crying, I don't think, but the relief and happiness that fills me up breaks off the part of my pessimism that told me this was too far away to even dream about.

Jeannette holds out her hand for me to shake, sealing our deal. I don't have an ounce of decorum in me as I throw myself into her arms, letting loose a cry of elation on her shoulder.

I will have a kitchen to help make my dreams come true.

There is nothing in the world that could tether me back to reality now. I am off in my dreamland, conjuring up happy images of my bakery come to life.

Marianne scrubs the tears off her cheeks. "I think that means we'll take it."

Breathless, I fall to my knees, wondering how it came to be that life decided to treat me so kind. Sweetwater Falls is my home, and a giant piece of my heart.

A LITTLE HELP FROM MY FRIENDS

J haven't stopped floating since I left Sweetwater Fountains yesterday. The contract was apparently nothing Marianne's "not my" boyfriend couldn't handle in an hour, making everything official last night. I barely slept, smiling so broad, I could hardly reason with my body's need for a REM cycle.

This morning, I bounce from room to room, humming like a bird on the first day of spring. Winifred laughs at my jovial antics as I dance into the kitchen, unbothered by guilt when the mess greets me. "Have no fear, Aunt Winnie. A cleaning service will be here this afternoon. By the time I get all my stuff out and she scrubs down the house, it will be as if I never took over your kitchen."

Winnie shakes her head through her smile. "Now, you know that's not necessary. I am perfectly capable of cleaning my own kitchen."

PEPPERMINT PERIL | 151

"Yes, but this will get it back to perfect. Plus, it's my way of saying thank you for letting me bake here for so long, and for lying through your teeth when you told me it didn't bother you one bit."

"It didn't!" Winifred insists. "I like having you in my space. I know it's selfish, but I'll be lonely with you out of the house during the day. I'll miss my kitchen smelling like sugar."

I kiss her cheek. "I'm going to be at my new baking space all day, scrubbing it down and doing what I can to get it ready to use. Do you need a ride to Karen's?" They've been talking about getting together today to bake their signature fruit cakes. I have no idea what makes a fruit cake someone's signature dessert, since I've always loathed the things, but to each their own.

Winifred stands, rinsing her teacup out in the sink. "That would be lovely, honey cake. It's too cold to go in the golf cart."

"Absolutely." I help Winifred with her jacket, grateful that she lets me drive her places and assist her with the little things.

It is the best feeling in the world to drop off Winifred at Karen's and then drive to Strawberry Street. I have my own parking spot now behind Sweetwater Fountains. I have no idea how Jeannette found the time to do this, but she even put a sign on the parking spot with my name on it, and one for Marianne, as well. It's the little things that feel like big things. The first task I do when I get out of the car is take a picture of the nameplate.

Contracts are fine and dandy, but having a parking space with my name on it? Now I know I work here.

I didn't expect Marianne to be here, but her car is a welcome sight, indeed. The prospect of a deep clean has never been particularly appealing before, but this morning, it feels like the first step on my road to true bliss. I tug the cleaning supplies out of the trunk, complete with a bucket and a solution I found at the Colonel's General Store. It promises to get out any stain or spot of stubborn grease.

I know that after I get the inventory cleared out of the kitchen, I will need every ounce in these bottles to make the place shine.

I don't have my keys yet, but the backdoor is propped open, so I slip inside with my bucket of cleaning accoutrement and make my way to the kitchen. My brows furrow when I hear two men talking. When I round the corner and take in the sight of Logan and Carlos holding boxes, I drop the bucket in surprise. "What are you doing here?"

Logan's shoulders fall. "You weren't supposed to be here for another hour. I thought you had something at the house and you were going to call Marianne before you came here."

"I wanted to surprise her by getting started early, so she didn't have to do as much work."

Marianne speaks from behind me. "We had the same idea, but earlier. I've been here since midnight, and Logan and Carlos came around one in the morning."

I gape at the three of them, horrified and honored that they gave up sleep to help lug around boxes from the kitchen into the storage room for Jeannette. "You did what?"

Logan is too tired to care about decorum. He shuffles over to me and tugs me into a hug, kissing my cheek. "Coffee has no impact on me anymore. But look! It's almost finished. This is the last haul of Jeanette's stuff, and then we can start shining this place up."

He's right. There are three boxes left. I could only picture with my imagination how spectacular the kitchen looked beneath the many boxes and crates of goods. To see the stoves, the industrial fridge, the long expanse of floor, the countertops with plenty of space... My imagination goes into hyperdrive, filling in the spots with every kind of cupcake imaginable.

"I can't believe you guys did this." I bury my face in Logan's chest. "I don't know what to say. This is incredible."

Carlos grins at us. "Miss out on an opportunity to move this many boxes? Not a chance. I sit in an office all day long. It was nice to move around like this. Plus, I get to feel like I'm a part of something." He extends his arm in Marianne's direction, and sure enough, she trots to his side. "But I'm going to crash hard on your couch when we're finished. That was the other half of the appeal to drive two hours to get here in the middle of the night. I don't like going a full week without seeing my girlfriend up close."

My grin elevates my entire posture. Marianne has been very clear that Carlos is not her boyfriend up until this point. I'm so glad they made things official.

This truly is a magical kitchen.

Marianne nuzzles Carlos' nose, which is just about the cutest sight I have ever seen.

"Put me to work," I offer. "Should I go to the storage room and start organizing things for Jeannette?"

"No need," Marianne replies. "We installed shelves for her and labeled everything, so it's all organized for her. Now it's just cleaning things up so everything is sanitary, and then we start plugging appliances in to see if they work."

Logan's hands are clumsy as he rubs my back. "Bill is coming over in two hours to help us with all the gas line stuff that I don't want to learn about. He's going to make sure the appliances work so we don't blow anything up in the process."

"I'm still processing how this all happened overnight. You three are amazing."

"Not just us," Marianne adds, leaning on Carlos' arm. "Winnie told Karen and Agnes, so they started sewing us aprons in the same colors as our delivery boxes. Same color as the logo." Then she grimaces. "That was supposed to be a surprise. Oops."

"I take it they didn't need to meet up to make their

signature fruit cakes?" I shake my head. "I can't believe I fell for that." I chuckle at the team spirit surrounding me and the love that fills my heart. "Then it looks like I can make myself useful cleaning for now."

It's easier said than done, because much of the grease is more than a decade old. But the Colonel's General Store cleaning solution doesn't lie, because it lifts up much of the stuff on the first swipe if I let it sit on the stained surfaces for five minutes first.

It takes the entire two hours until Bill arrives for us to finish with our deep clean. My nails are ground to nubs, my arms ache from the repetitive scrubbing motion, and my knees creak when I stand to greet Bill. "Thanks for coming to help us with this, Bill."

My former boss when I was a waitress at Bill's Diner has only one mood: surly. Today is no exception. "Yeah, yeah. Can't have you blowing things up back here because something doesn't get hooked up properly."

Carlos and Marianne are hovering by the exit. I can tell they are anxious to get back to Marianne's house to wash up and crash from their all-nighter. They've been doing the heavy lifting to make my dreams come true.

Logan leans against the fridge he just finished scrubbing clean with baking soda, his arms draped heavily over my shoulders while I lean my back to his chest. If he fell asleep standing up, I would not be surprised.

Bill does a lot of grumbling and fidgeting with cords, but eventually, he gets the stove working with zero explosions to speak of. The fridge works but is in need of a new fridge lightbulb. The exhaust fan needs a cleaning service to come out and do a quality inspection of its innerworkings. But other than that, Bill can't find anything to complain about, which is saying something.

When he shuffles out, waving off my cheery gratitude, relief spreads through me. "We did it. After we get the exhaust fan cleaned out, we can actually open in here."

Logan squeezes my hand. "I'll make some calls today and set that up."

I tilt my head at him. "You don't have to do that. This is my business. The headaches should be mine."

Logan smirks at me, his eyes lidded with impending sleep. "I thought the point of us was to make sure headaches were limited or nonexistent. I like helping, Miss Charlotte. All you have to do is let me."

I am fairly certain I am the luckiest girl in the world.

21

EMILY'S CLEANING SERVICE

*W*hen Carlos, Marianne, Logan and I pack up from cleaning out the industrial kitchen, Jeannette meets me with my keys and a hug, making her officially the greatest landlord ever.

The others go to their houses to shower, and I assume to take the longest naps ever, which is my plan for the afternoon before I pick up Winifred from Karen's house. I will try to act surprised when the Live Forever Club presents me with handmade aprons that match the pink of my logo perfectly.

Yet another bit of proof that I live in the greatest town in the world.

My feet are dragging when I get into my car and drive toward the house, but my spirits are soaring over a job well done and the prospect of a shower that was hard earned.

Emily is most likely in the middle of shining up the house to make it all sparkly and new. I left her an envelope with her payment and a thank you note on the kitchen table, so hopefully I can slip into the shower without bothering her.

But my plans for peace are shattered when I pull into the driveway, parking right behind a blue sedan with a cracked back window.

My heartrate speeds up. This is the car that was at Nick and Nancy's party. It left as we pulled up. This is the guest that was unaccounted for because none of the guests own a car matching this description.

My mouth feels like sand when I call Logan and leave a quick message on his voicemail. "Hey, the blue sedan is at my house. It belongs to the housekeeper I hired for the day to shine up the place as a thank you to Aunt Winnie. Logan, she was there the day of the Christmas party, but Nick and Nancy didn't mention her." My mouth pulls to the side. "She exited out the side door. Maybe they didn't see her? I'm not sure. I'm going inside. I'll ask her if she was there the day of the party. If she tells the truth, she has nothing to hide. If she lies... Call me when you get this."

I end the call and unbuckle my seatbelt against my better judgment. Maybe I should wait for Logan. Then again, just because the housekeeper's car was there doesn't mean Emily of Emily's Cleaning Service is guilty of murder.

It just means that she was at Nick and Nancy's the

night of the murder without invite or appointment, and without the homeowner knowing she was in the house.

I'm sure there's a logical explanation for her being there. I'll talk with her and find out why she was there, so the sheriff can cross Emily off the list of suspects. Same thing I did with Marcus.

I can do this. No big deal.

When I walk into the house, I am greeted by the same thin layer of dust that was here when I left. Maybe she just got started. "Emily?" I call through the house as I move through the living room toward the kitchen.

I hear a scramble across the linoleum. I expect to see her with a mop in her hands or something, but when my eyes take in the unscrubbed kitchen, all I see is a pen in her hand and a piece of paper on the table.

"You're home early," she accuses, as if I've done something wrong. She brushes her chin-length inky hair out of her face, revealing a pinched nose and a sour expression, as if I barged in on her in the bathroom.

I grimace. "Sorry about that. Yeah, I thought my errand would take the whole of the day, but I had some help, so we finished way early. I'll get out of your hair."

"Yes. Thank you."

Her behavior is oddly squirrely, her body tense as she moves to block my view of the table as I set my purse on the counter.

"Is everything okay?"

"Of course. Why wouldn't it be?" Her voice is high-

pitched and squeaky, like she's been caught doing something wrong.

I move around her so I can check the table. "I left your
envelope here with your payment. Did you get it?"

"Uh-huh, I..."

But the envelope isn't there. In its place is my thank
you letter, open on the table with a piece of paper beside it
that I didn't write. I squint at the printing as I pick it up,
ignoring her protest that I should go on a walk and leave
her alone to clean. "This looks like my handwriting on a
bad day, only I didn't write this." The words smack me in
the face with their potency as I read them aloud.

"'TOM,

YOU SHOULD HAVE KNOWN NOT TO CROSS ME.

-CHARLOTTE'"

I GLANCE UP FROM THE LETTER, CONFUSED AND HORRIFIED
that something like this could be sitting on my table.
"What did..."

But I don't get my sentence out before Emily flings her

thin yet muscular body at me. Her eyes widen with pure insanity. "You weren't supposed to be here!"

Then Emily grabs a pan from the sink and swings it at me, missing my head but smashing it across my ribs.

My body slams into the counter, along with the realization that I hired Tom's killer to clean my home.

22

DIRTY MURDER

*E*mily was supposed to clean the house for us. She came recommended by Nick and Nancy. This one luxury was going to show Aunt Winnie how much I appreciate her generosity. I came home early from cleaning the industrial kitchen in the back room of Sweetwater Fountains only to find Emily copying my handwriting to try and frame me for Tom's murder.

My ribs ache with the sting from where she bashed me in the side with the frying pan. I stumble away, using the length of the countertop to keep me upright. "Why?" I manage, truly perplexed more than angry that this stranger would pin a murder on me. "I don't even know you!"

The wild gleam in Emily's brown eyes tells me she doesn't care about the logic that has missed her actions. "Don't you see? That's what makes it perfect."

"What are you talking about?" I can't find anything heavy enough to do real damage, or anything with which to defend myself until my eyes fall on the knife block.

I really don't want to do this.

But when Emily advances, swinging her arms up and bringing the frying pan down with the intent of bashing me in the head to knock me out, I know I have no other choice. My body rings with pain when I hold my arm up to shield my head from taking the brunt of the blow. My ribs protest the movement, but I manage to narrowly avoid a concussion when the frying pan cracks down across my forearm.

Emily's shout is shrill. "Tom was supposed to pay me for Nick and Nancy's job! They told me he would!"

I grimace when I tug the biggest cleaver we have out of the knife block, wishing for a weapon that doesn't look like it's already been used to murder someone. "So you killed him?"

"I didn't mean to! I only wanted the money I was owed. I lost my temper. I'm so sick of being jerked around. You don't know what it's like to do a huge job like that and get paid nothing. Nothing!" She swings the frying pan at my fist now, but I hold tight to the knife, so I don't drop it when she bashes my knuckles.

I cry out in agony, knowing I don't have it in me to actually stab someone, even if it's to save my own life. "Why are you attacking me? I paid you before you even started the job!"

Tears prick her eyes now. "I needed someone to take the focus off me. The police called me to ask where I was the day the body was discovered. They were onto me! They probably saw me hauling in the body just before the party started. No one was supposed to see!"

Nick and Nancy weren't lying. They cleaned their house themselves before the party started, but Emily slipped the body in through the side door when they were otherwise occupied. Had Marianne and I arrived at the house a minute earlier—had I not driven below the speed limit to get there for fear of wrecking my cupcakes—we would have caught her in the act.

I keep the knife between us. "Why dump the body at Nick and Nancy's? Why involve them in this mess?"

Emily's eyes are round with agony. "Because either Tom was stiffing me for the job, or they were. So one of them dies, and the other will hang for it."

"But you wrote up a confession note with my name on it!"

"Because the police didn't arrest Nick and Nancy, like they were supposed to!"

I don't want to hurt this clearly disturbed woman. I don't want to use the knife that I switch to my unbruised hand.

Buttercream swims in the fishbowl two feet from where I stand, flicking her tail at the violence that is unfolding before her goldfish eyes.

She is too young to have to see brutality like this.

I throw my body into Emily's. I don't stop until she is pinned against the far wall. But the victory is short-lived. She is stronger than she looks. She shoves me off her, swinging her fist out to clock me across the jaw.

I am unskilled at fighting, but luckily the meat cleaver in my fist doesn't need me for much. My arm flies out, slicing a bloody line across her thigh that draws a scream from her lips. I lunge for my purse, since that is where my phone is.

But my back turned to Emily is a poor plan.

I jerk to the side a split second before the frying pan cuts through the air, narrowly missing my body.

The crash of glass and splash of water are the last things I hope to hear.

Buttercream.

A bloodcurdling scream erupts from me when my sweet fish's bowl crashes to the kitchen floor, shattering and leaving my baby to fend for itself too far out of its element. "No!" I cry out for my fish, wondering what kind of monster could possibly want to kill an innocent baby who's done nothing wrong in her entire life. "How could you?"

Though, as I say this, it occurs to me that a person who murdered a man might not have any scruples left concerning a fish.

But this is *my* fish. My fish that Logan won me at the Twinkle Lights Festival. This is my little baby that I managed to keep alive for months, which is an all-time record for me.

Rage rises up in me, covering over the fact that I am not a fighter and have no idea what I'm doing. I charge across the kitchen and throw myself at Emily, knocking the frying pan out of her hand while Buttercream flops around on the floor, silently calling out for her mommy to save her.

"You killed Tom!" I cry, pummeling Emily to the floor and punching her across the face.

"Get off me!"

I keep my knees fastened on either side of her hips as I lean to the side, grasping for the frying pan that has caused me so much pain. Emily's hands coil around my neck, squeezing hard enough to make my eyes bug. With my free hand, I struggle against her grip, trying to pry even one of her fingers off my throat to no avail. My grip on the frying pan is flimsy, but it's my last hope for survival.

My swing isn't nearly as hard as it should be, but with the last puff of breath in my lungs, I crack the frying pan to the side of Emily's head, loosening her grip once and for all.

23

BACKUP

*T*he relief of air is short-lived as it fills my lungs. I can still feel the phantom pressure of Emily's fingers digging into my throat, even though her arms are now limp at her sides.

The first thing I should do is make a dash for my phone to call the police, but my heart has been wrung dry, bleeding for Buttercream who is still flopping on the floor, silently calling for me to help set her world right again.

I sob as I fill a cup with tepid water, making sure it is not too hot or cold. Then I scoop up my baby, accidentally slicing my already bruised knuckle on a shard of glass from her bowl.

Her home.

I invited someone inside who broke my baby's home.

Apologies will never be enough, but I can't stop spilling them from my lips as I return Buttercream to the

water. I don't breathe until I see her tail flick with gratitude, though it should be judgment. I hired Emily. I
didn't think it through. The pieces were right in front of
me this entire time, yet I still couldn't see what was
obvious.

My fingers are clumsy as I tug my phone out of my
purse and call the precinct, speaking in choppy sentences
to the dispatcher. After I rattle off my address and request
police to take away Tom's killer, I call Logan. This time, he
picks up before the voicemail can kick on. "Emily was in
all three places."

"What? Charlotte, are you okay? You sound upset."

I called him in the middle of something, I can tell, but I
can't even conjure up an apology; I am so scattered. "Emily
went to Tom's house. Then she cleaned Nick and Nancy's.
She wasn't scheduled to clean the day of the party, but her
car was there! Why would she come just before a party
starts to clean a house? The clues were right in front of me
the whole time!"

"Slow down. What clues? Are you okay?"

"I hired Emily! She was supposed to clean the house
while I was at the fountain!"

"What fountain?"

I motion with my free hand, grimacing at the pain of
any movement. I truly hope my arm isn't broken. My ribs
ache with each breath, large or small. "Sweetwater Fountains! I was there today while Emily was here. The letter,
Logan! She wrote my letter!"

"I'm putting on my shoes and coming over. Emily wrote your letter? What does that mean? What letter?"

"Come over," I breathe, my hand shaking from adrenaline. "There's blood."

I hear the roar of Logan's truck. "Are you bleeding? Charlotte, hang up and call an ambulance."

"Not me. I cut Emily's thigh with a meat cleaver! She's on the floor, Logan. Hurry!" I don't want to hit her again if she wakes up before the police get here, but I know that is what I will have to do.

"I'm on my way. Did you call the precinct?"

"Yes. They're sending people." I work out a staccato breath. "You. You're my people."

Logan's voice comes back gentle. "That's right. I am your people, and I'm on my way. Hold on, Miss Charlotte. It sounds like you did the heavy lifting already. All you have to do is wait for me to get there, and you can take a break."

Tears prick my cheeks as I stand over Emily's supine form. She hasn't roused yet, but I know it could happen at any moment.

By the time the police get to my house, my fist has formed around the handle of the knife so much that the sheriff has to carefully pry it from my fingers.

"Easy," he says in a soothing voice. "Wayne, help me with Charlotte. Bag everything. What is this?" He looks at the letter. "I take it you didn't write this."

I shake my head, which is the most communication I

can muster just yet. I point to Emily with a shaking hand. "Framed me."

The sheriff hangs his head. I can tell the sheriff is working through the obvious clues that we didn't bother connecting in the beginning. "Tom's body was found at Nick and Nancy's, where Emily worked."

"She wasn't scheduled that day," I add, bringing to light a key bit of evidence that I had previously overlooked as unfortunate happenstance. "I hired her to clean here."

"Instead of cleaning, she tried to set you up for Tom's murder. I'm guessing that's because we called her this week to ask her whereabouts the day of the murder. She needed us off her trail."

I am shaking, my body aching as I try to keep my head in the game. I don't want to completely lose my composure.

The sheriff cups my shoulder and leans in to meet my gaze. "The ambulance is on its way, kiddo. You hang in there."

My lower lip trembles with guilt. "I cut Emily. It was self-defense, but I sliced open her thigh and I hit her in the head with the frying pan once I wrestled it away from her."

The sheriff nods, absolving my hemorrhaging conscience with a solemn nod. "She's not going to bleed out." He glances over his shoulder. "Wayne's already bandaged up her leg, so she will recover. Hopefully with a little more sense in her when she wakes up."

"I... I..." I manage, unsure how to finish my sentence.

The sheriff's thick salt and pepper eyebrows smooth out as he takes in my quaking form. His squared, dimpled jaw firms with things I can tell he wants to say to me, but isn't sure how. Finally his shoulders lower. "It's going to be okay now, Charlotte." He opens up one arm to me, inviting me in for a careful hug.

I don't hesitate to let him steady me, but sink into the embrace. I let his promise cover over my sore spots, grateful for the support.

The sheriff walks me over to the nearest chair and pulls it out for me. "You just sit here and focus on breathing. We'll take care of the rest."

The sheriff takes pictures of everything while making sure not to leave my side until the sound of Logan's voice fills the house. "Charlotte? Charlotte!" He races into the kitchen, scooping me up in a hug that crushes my already bruised ribs. "Tell me everything. Tell me you're okay."

The sheriff pries his son off me and lowers me back down into my seat. "She was in a fight, Logan. Easy, Son."

Logan thumbs my cheeks as both compassion and true worry radiate out from him. "Marianne is on her way. I called Winifred but told her to stay put in case the house was in such disarray that it might traumatize her."

I lean forward, taking the shoulder he offers as he bends down to hug me in a less painful manner. The smell of his cologne centers the chaotic parts inside of me that might never calm down otherwise.

"What can I do?" Logan asks me. Being that his father

and his partner are directing the medics to take Emily out of the house, there is precious little for him to do until he has been filled in on the details.

"Buttercream's bowl shattered," I work out, my chin wobbling with emotion I cannot contain. "Can you make sure she's okay?"

Logan doesn't question my sanity but glances at the counter to the water glass. "She's okay, but how about I get her a bigger bowl. I don't think the cup is wide enough for her to stay in for long."

I nod, but don't let him get up. Instead of leaning back so he can stand and tend to the goldfish, I curve my good arm around his shoulders, taking this slice of a moment to rest my forehead in the crook of his neck. My tears fall onto his collar, and with them goes the brunt of my worry.

No matter what happens in life, today has made me sure that I will never have to tackle the big things on my own. I have backup, if only I can remember to wait for them to come.

24

CHRISTMAS HEIST

*K*aren's green gelatin dessert is a scientific wonder. It is chunky in spots and cloudy in others as it jiggles on the counter, free of its mold. If I didn't know better, I would guess there was cottage cheese mixed in there, along with pineapple and I can't guess what else. I don't want to taste it, but I know that won't be an option once dessert is served.

For once, I was not in charge of desserts, which is just as well. Apparently, Karen's big thing is making this weird green gelatin every Christmas Eve. I'm glad not to step on her toes, but rather fold myself into their traditional holiday meal with my own flare.

"It is decided that Charlotte will always be in charge of rolls on Christmas Eve," Agnes declares, raising her glass of wassail.

Karen and Marianne raise their glasses to toast me while Winifred claps her hands and Logan whistles merrily.

I snicker at the praise. "You guys, they're just rolls."

Marianne guffaws. "Are you kidding me? These are not 'just rolls.' You made them to look like cupcakes! And what is inside of this? It's pork and some kind of fancy cheese."

"Divine, is what it is," Agnes rules.

I can't help but smile. "Buttermilk rolls baked in a cupcake pan, stuffed with pork and brie, glazed with garlic butter and piped mashed potatoes on top. The sprinkles are chives."

Logan points to his half-eaten roll on his plate. "These are the fanciest rolls I've ever eaten." Then he looks around the table at the women. "I haven't heard ample praise for my cranberry sauce. I know you're impressed with my can opening skills. Don't hold back on my account."

Winifred laughs at his antics. "Oh, my. I didn't realize you'd brought the cranberry sauce, Logan. I thought for sure it was sent here from the heavens."

Karen toasts him. "Very cranberry-y."

Logan snickers. "That's what I was going for."

We all talk and laugh animatedly as we eat until we are groaning. Then we take a break to decorate the Christmas tree that Marianne and I set up earlier this week in the living room.

I bring Buttercream out in the new bowl Logan bought

me for Christmas, which is a few inches bigger than the one that broke. Now wherever I go in the house, I bring my fish along for the ride. After seeing her flopping around, fighting for her life, I don't have the heart to leave her alone in the kitchen while I move about the house.

"I've never had a real Christmas tree before," I comment as I pop open the box of shiny red and silver bulbs. "It smells like a hug. We should be writing letters to Santa underneath it."

Agnes busies about with the tinsel while Logan, Marianne and I hang the ornaments. Winifred turns on Christmas music from the Rat Pack, bringing a sense of togetherness while Karen sips her wassail on the couch. The presents under the tree look that much more appealing, now that the lights are strung and the ornaments dot the greenery. The whole thing looks like a Christmas card, smack in the middle of a holiday movie.

Once we are finished and sitting around with our wassail that has most certainly been spiked with something decadent to calm us all down for the night, Marianne starts poking at the Christmas presents until Agnes calls for her to pass them out.

In all the hubbub of murder and mayhem, I worried that my mission to pick out the perfect Christmas gifts would suffer. But when I stopped by the craft store to buy more sucker sticks for the cake pops, I realized Jeannette was right: when I was ready, the perfect gifts came to me.

Karen whistles her approval when she tugs out a sexy

silk cami and shorts pajama set that I know she will like, since she owns something similar in a different color. The red in Logan's cheeks is quite an amusing sight.

Agnes squeals when she unwraps a book of bikini knitting patterns, swearing up and down that we should all expect knitted bikinis for Christmas next year. "I'm in the book club, and we've all been knitting up a storm lately."

Marianne studies the amethyst gemstones in the base of her new fountain, her eyes widening when I explain why Jeannette selected the pretty purple stones to bring a soothing quality into the library and increase focus. Hopefully with this fountain, people will enjoy their stay at her establishment that much more.

Before Winifred opens her gift, she stares at the wrapping with a tinge of sadness in her glassy green eyes. "I feel terrible, knowing that Nick and Nancy are alone this year. Their party was ruined. And hardly any children wanted to come sit on Santa's lap at the Christmas Festival because of how it all went down with Tom, and them not paying their housekeeper. And poor Tom. He was too young to have died like that." She sighs at the box in her hand. "I'm happy it's Christmas, but the whole holiday seems tainted somehow. I don't know how to scrub all of the awful happenings from my mind so we can enjoy our Christmas Eve."

I know the feeling. While I have enjoyed every minute of our dinner, a slow sadness has been creeping over my shoulder because Tom's death didn't need to be.

Suddenly, I stand, making a decision to set things right as much as I am able. "I have to run an errand."

Agnes sits straighter, blinking at me. "Now? Nothing's open, dear. It's Christmas Eve."

"I have unfinished business to settle."

Marianne stands. "I'm coming with you."

"Me, too!" the others chime in. They don't even know what I'm up to, but they don't want to be separated even for a few minutes on Christmas Eve.

Maybe we all have a little unfinished business to see to tonight.

We pile into my car, with Logan driving and Marianne sitting on my lap in the passenger's seat while the Live Forever Club takes up the back. I instruct Logan to drive to Delia's house. He doesn't bat an eye as he steps on the gas.

The drive is short, so I don't have time to talk myself out of this stroke of bravery that might not be entirely necessary.

When Logan pulls into Delia's driveway, I notice a car parked on the street. "She's got company," I comment, wishing I could tie up this loose end without additional witnesses.

Logan nods. "That's Frank's car. Frank is spending Christmas Eve with Delia?"

"They're dating. Well, they're just starting to date." It's all the explanation I give before I am out of the car with Marianne by my side. We march up to the front porch with

Logan and the Live Forever Club shuffling behind us as I ring the doorbell.

When Delia opens the door and takes in the sight of six people crammed on her front porch, her surprise is genuine. "Hey, guys. Merry Christmas. What's up?"

"You have something in your house that doesn't belong here," I blurt out, marching past her without an invitation to enter.

Delia protests, turning with her upper lip curled, her frizzy chestnut hair bobbing in a ponytail atop her head. "Hey, I didn't ask you to come inside. What are you doing, Charlotte?"

Winifred is quick on her feet. "We're caroling!" Then she starts singing a loud rendition of *Happy Birthday* in her beautiful cabaret voice, clearly forgetting that *Happy Birthday* is not a traditional caroling song.

But Agnes, Karen, Marianne and Logan all follow suit, singing along as I stomp through the house, finding Frank standing up from the couch in the front room. "Hey, Frank. Merry Christmas."

Frank tilts his head at me. "What's going on, Charlotte?"

"Oh, just looking for..." My eyes land on Delia's hearth, taking in the sight of a dozen tall nutcracker soldiers, lined up in front of her fireplace as if she purchased them to go with her Christmas décor.

But she didn't purchase them. She stole them.

I march up to the hearth and yank down two at a time, piling the tall, awkward things in my arm.

Delia squawks at me. "Charlotte, leave my nutcrackers alone!"

"They're not yours, and you know it."

"You know what I mean. Nick and Nancy don't care that I sneak a couple away every year at their party. They have hundreds."

"Even though Nancy is not my favorite person in the world right now, Tom's entire murder started out with dishonesty and a simple misunderstanding. It all could have been avoided and maybe Tom would still be alive if the two of them hadn't tried to scam Tom into footing Emily's payment. They were all small, selfish lies in the beginning, but we've all seen how they can spiral out of control. These nutcrackers are going back to their rightful home tonight."

Delia harrumphs at me. "I'm not a real thief, Charlotte. You are so dramatic! No one is going to murder anyone over a nutcracker or two."

"How about twelve nutcrackers?" I gather them all up in my arms, unsure if this is the best way to transport them without risking a ding here or there on the fragile paint.

My forearm is still bruised from Emily's attack, but I fight through the wince that might have me back down. I can't bring Tom back from the dead, but this is a wrong I can right tonight.

I tip my head in Frank's direction. "See you around, Frank."

Delia's hands on her hips tell me she will not forgive me for calling her out on this.

I don't care.

When she opens her mouth to yell at me, I don't back down. "Did you throw chocolate into Tom's yard to try and hurt Beanie?"

Delia's pause before her scandalized gasp is telling. "I would never."

Uh-huh.

I stomp out of her house to the tune of *Happy Birthday*, carrying my recovered contraband to my car where I shove it into the trunk. "Pile in, people. Santa's got a delivery to make. It's Christmas Eve, so we should get going."

Winifred laughs at the scandal of me basically robbing Delia of her stolen goods. And I did it without backup, other than carol singers who couldn't even manage a proper Christmas song.

It's a short trip to Nick and Nancy's house, but I am breathless the whole way. "I can't believe I just did that. I marched into her house and took all her stolen nutcrackers." I cover my mouth with my hand. "Did I really do that?"

Marianne giggles with delight. "You sure did! I'm so glad I insisted on tagging along. That was incredible! Delia was spitting mad. Hilarious!"

Logan pulls into Nick and Nancy's driveway, but instead of announcing our presence, we decide to line up the nutcrackers on the front porch, so when they open the door, the little soldiers are there to greet them.

Whiskers, their cat, watches us curiously from the window, silently asking if I have gone insane, no doubt.

Honestly, her guess is as good as mine, but I've never felt more alive than I do now.

Karen scrawls in her perfect calligraphy on a scrap piece of paper she found in my car.

"*SEE THAT YOU AREN'T SO NAUGHTY NEXT YEAR.*

LOVE, SANTA"

OUR LAUGHTER CAN BARELY BE CONTAINED WHEN I WAIT FOR my friends to load themselves into the car before I ring the doorbell. After I push the button, I race to the car and Logan speeds down the driveway, making a quick getaway before Nick and Nancy open their front door and find their stolen goods returned.

"I love spending Christmas with you all," Logan comments on the way home. "Next year, can we knock over a liquor store or something? I think all holidays should come with a little theft. I'm always doing the cop thing. I never get to help make robberies happen."

I reach over and hold his hand, grateful for this group that makes each day feel like the best one ever. Last year, I spent the holidays alone in my apartment, watching bad television and wishing I was bold enough to put myself out there and make some real friends.

One year later, and I have turned into Charlotte the Brave, stealing toys and righting old wrongs.

When we pile into the house, Karen insists on doling out the chunky green gelatin concoction, which actually isn't bad at all. It's got a fruity sort of pineapple taste to it, even if the texture is revolting.

The glow of Christmas cheer surrounds my aunt when she opens a gift certificate for a family portrait. I made an appointment for us to go together in two weeks. "What is this?" she asks.

"It's for the two of us. We need a family portrait done to show people that two adorable goofballs live here together."

Winifred holds the gift certificate over her heart, truly touched that we are about to add something personal and precious to the home we share with much love and kindness.

In the end, I know that there is no place I would rather be than here with my family—those of my genetics and those of my choosing. They made my dreams their own, and in return, my heart belongs to them.

The End.

Love the book?
Leave a review!

Caramel Corruption is book six in the Cupcake Crimes series. Enjoy a free preview now:

Good Friend, Old Flame

I was stifling my groans an hour ago when we were moving the furniture into Carlos' new office, but after unloading the millionth box of legal briefs from the moving truck, I don't hold back. "Ugh. I think I pulled a muscle."

Marianne's brows pinch together. "Which one?"

"All of them."

Marianne snickers as she sets down a large box beside mine on the long, oval table. The walls are a boring white and the floor is a honey-colored wood. I sure hope one of these boxes has decorations in them.

Marianne swipes the sweat off her brow as she grins up

at me. "Have I mentioned how grateful I am that you're helping me move Carlos into his new office?"

"You did. Have I mentioned how happy I am that your boyfriend doesn't live two hours away anymore?"

Marianne is still new to the idea of referring to the big city lawyer as her boyfriend. Her neck shrinks as the tips of her ears turn pink. "Telling me his boss is putting him in charge of opening a new branch in Hamshire was quite the conversation. I timed the drive from my house to his office. Twenty-two minutes, Charlotte. We'll only be twenty-two minutes away from each other."

Carlos is still outside, but I lower my voice all the same. "You sure it's okay with you? You would tell him if it was moving too fast, right?"

Marianne starts stacking the boxes to make room for more. "We've been dating, doing the phone thing for a few months now. It's a big step, but I like it." She smiles, her short brown hair swishing across her chin. "I like him. Doesn't make me guess as to what he's thinking. Doesn't make me worry he's cheating." Her expression tightens, so I know she is thinking about Jeremy—the man she was with for years, who ended their engagement by cheating on her. "Carlos is a good man. He treats me like I'm special."

"That's because you are special." Before I can keep my true feelings inside, a shadow crosses over my mood. "Have I told you lately how much I loathe your ex-fiancé? I never met the guy, but to have put you through a long-distance relationship while he was cheating on you... I'm glad Carlos is a solid guy."

"Me, too. Living only twenty-two minutes away from him will be nice. The drive was a real drain." Her eyebrows dance. "Now we can double date more often."

"I like the sound of that. What's the next town event?" My mouth pulls to the side while I stretch my arms over my head. "Or does Sweetwater Falls take a break from town festivals during the winter months?"

Marianne chuckles as Carlos comes in with another giant box of... I'm guessing important lawyerly things. "Oh, no. We just move the events indoors. In a couple of weeks, there's the Knit Your Heart Out fair."

Carlos tilts his head to the side, wiping his forehead with the back of his hand. Though he usually wears a crisp suit or nice business casual clothing, today this man in his forties is in jeans and a polo, with a winter hat covering his dark hair. Even after spending all morning lifting heavy things, his posture is still perfect. "Knit Your Heart Out? That sounds like it would only happen in Sweetwater Falls," Carlos comments with a winded smile. "I'm in."

I love the sound of everything in Sweetwater Falls. Back when I lived in a big city, if I had heard of an event with that title, I wouldn't think twice, but in the sweet small town I adore, suddenly I can't think of anything cuter than a fair to celebrate knitting. "Let's get tickets to that, for sure. Is it like, people knit blankets and sell them for charity?"

Marianne giggles at what I thought was a solid guess. "Ho, no. I mean, sure, there are blankets. But it's so much more fun than that. The local book club, As the Page Turns, puts on the fair every January to raise money for their book club. They knit all sorts of crazy things. It's a blast. No matter how many items are for sale, they sell out every year."

I rack my brain for different things a person could knit. "Blankets, winter hats, mittens. What else?"

Marianne plops down on one of the chairs. Her arms flop over the arms of the seat, her legs sprawled because it's been that long of a day. "Stuffed animals, of course. Sweaters. They knit potholders, ties, tea cozies, slippers, socks with funny sayings on them. Then there's a whole section of cross-stitch stuff. One year, they auctioned off a cross-stitch piece that was a picture of Rip, the Town Selectman, sitting on the toilet. Sold for two hundred dollars. I'm still mad I got outbid."

My eyes bug. "Whoa! That's pretty cool. I didn't realize you could do so much with yarn. The Live Forever Club has been knitting more than usual this week. I should pay closer attention to what they're making." I roll my eyes at myself. "I am useless with knitting needles."

Marianne grins at me. "Don't let Agnes hear you say that. She'll make it her mission to educate you."

Carlos picks up Marianne's arm and massages her wrist. His skin is a few shakes darker than her olive hue. They are so cute together. "I love that it won't be a two-hour drive to go to the town events anymore. I have never been more excited to go to a knitting fair."

Marianne's eyes close at the pampering. "I'm so glad you're moving to Hamshire. That's so close."

Carlos jerks his thumb to the front door of the office. "My stuff is moved into my condo. That's the last of the boxes for the office. The sign is hanging outside. Now it's just a matter of unpacking and setting things up. Then I'm officially here."

"I love it." Marianne might start drooling if Carlos keeps massaging her wrist. "I am never leaving this conference room. Too tired."

When the front door of the office opens, the three of us blink at each other in confusion. "Is that your boyfriend, Charlotte?" Carlos asks me.

It's so strange that that is a legitimate question. I'm not used to being a girl who has a boyfriend. If it was anyone else, I might feel strange about it all, but as it's Logan, a smile toys with my lips whenever the topic of our relationship comes up.

I shake my head in Carlos' direction. "Logan is ice fishing with his dad this weekend." I motion to the spot where Carlos is joined to Marianne's wrist. "Keep up the good work. I'll play the role of receptionist."

I meander into the hallway, making my way to the receptionist's desk. The smooth surface has a computer that is not hooked up yet. There is a box of office supplies on the floor next to the chair.

I smile at the man standing in front of the desk. He is wearing cowboy boots that look new, paired with clean jeans and a pressed dress shirt tucked in. He is lean with long arms and legs, and looks like he's only ever worn cowboy western clothing for the fashion, and not for any actual ranch work.

I flash a breezy smile at the newcomer. "Hi, there. Welcome to Bankman and Voss. What can I help you with today?"

I am sweaty, despite the winter weather outside. My blonde curls have been slapped into a messy ponytail. My knitted lavender cardigan and jeans make me look less than professional, but my tone says that I am cool, calm and in control of this new office.

The man reaches out his hand to shake mine, cluing me in to the fact that he has clammy palms. Upon further inspection, he has a line of moisture dotting his forehead and cleanshaven upper lip. "I think I'm in need of some legal assistance." He motions to the nearly empty desk. "Are you folks open for business?"

He looks to be around my age and about the same height as my five-foot-ten-inches. "We're just getting this office set up, but there is a lawyer here who can take down your information, if you like."

The man nods eagerly, his coifed blond hair rustling with the motion. It is then that I notice a hint of panic wafting off him. "Yes, please. The sooner the better." He gestures with his hand for me to speed up. "Like, right now."

My eyes widen at his urgency, but I nod politely in response. "Yes, sir. Mister…"

"Mister Johnson."

"Just one moment, Mister Johnson."

I move back down the hallway, knocking once on the conference room door just in case the two lovebirds are mid-smooch.

I poke my head inside. "Carlos, you have your first client in the foyer."

Carlos grins. "I guess this was a hot spot to set up shop. Remind me to gloat to my boss that I was right."

Marianne stands to organize the boxes atop the table. "After your meeting with your first client, I vote we go out for lunch. I'm starved."

"Done. I need to get to know the restaurants around here. My boss is paying for lunch today, so pick somewhere nice."

I feather my fingers together. "Sushi with a side of sushi with sushi on top."

Carlos chuckles as he digs a legal pad out of one of the boxes. "Deal."

Marianne's nose scrunches. "I've never tried sushi before." Then a gleam takes over her insecurity that the Live Forever Club would deem as a Marianne the Wild sort of expression. "Let's do it!"

Carlos gives us a thumbs up before he exits, but after he's gone only a few seconds, I realize Carlos isn't fully prepared to greet a new client. "He doesn't have a pen," I tell Marianne, searching through the boxes for a writing instrument.

Marianne tugs a pencil out of her pocket. "I mean, I'm the Head Librarian. I think it's part of the uniform that I have a pencil on me at all times." She smirks at me and exits the room while I set my sights on at least getting the coffee cart set up in the conference room.

I don't get more than the coffeemaker out before I hear Marianne's voice turn shrill. "What are you doing here?"

Whether or not the situation warrants rushing, I dash out in the hallway toward Marianne. Anything that causes her the least bit of distress needs to be dealt with immediately.

As her best friend, that is my duty.

When I skid into the foyer, I don't see anything obviously alarming. Mister Johnson's eyes are wide, but he is a respectable conversational distance away from Carlos and Marianne. "Oh! Hi, Marianne. I didn't realize you... Do you work here? I assumed you were still at the library, shelving books."

I don't like the way he says, "shelving books." He might as well have said, "shoveling trash."

Marianne is mute, gaping at him with confusion radiating out from her. Her eyes are wide and her body language is taut with a fight-or-flight debate plain on her features.

Carlos motions between the two of them. "Do you two know each other?"

Marianne mouths a reply, but her volume has deserted her.

Mister Johnson supplies the answer that sends my heart plummeting. "We used to date." He shoves his hands in his pockets. "Actually, we used to be engaged."

My mouth hangs open. I am at a loss for words, which is just as well. Of all the things I have in me to say right now, most of them are unsavory swears. I have half a mind to march him straight out of here without further explanation.

Jeremy Johnson—A.K.A. the worst man in the world—has the gall to cast Marianne a sheepish smile. "Good to see you, sugarbean."

I am torn between vomiting at the stupid nickname and punching his lights out for invoking it after cheating on her like the slimeball he is.

Who on earth could possibly have the corroded soul to cheat on Marianne and break her heart? She is the most wonderful person in the world. She dreams in classic literature and always has time to help her neighbor.

Whatever led Jeremy to set foot in this law office, I am ready to ignore his issue and thrust him out the front door.

Carlos postures. "Marianne, why don't you go to the conference room and take a load off."

Marianne doesn't need more of an invitation to exit

than that. She disappears around the corner while I stand still, unable to move, lest I deck this man where he stands.

Carlos is ever the professional, though I can tell from his taut body language that he very much does not want this man in his office. "Tell me how the firm can help you, Mister Johnson."

I note clearly that Carlos said the firm can help Jeremy, and not that Carlos himself will be any part of helping his girlfriend's ex out of whatever jam he has created for himself with his shriveled heart and non-existent conscience.

Jeremy is still sweating as he jerks his chin toward the door. "It's better that I show you."

Carlos and I follow Jeremy out into the January air, shivering without our coats as we walk through the inch of unshoveled snow towards a newer black sedan.

It's a stupid car. For no reason other than that Jeremy drives it, I hate it and immediately deem it as pretentious.

Jeremy stands at the trunk, spreading his fingers out over the surface. "I'm a singer, see, on the American Pumpernickel tour. After the concert last night, I passed out in the tour bus. Usually my manager comes and wakes me up."

Because you're a child who can't take care of himself, I say to myself in a cruel manner.

I am never this mean, but this guy broke my best friend's heart. Therefore, he will forever be scum.

His cowboy boots are ridiculous. They have never been worn for actual ranching work, I'll bet.

Jeremy touches the top of the trunk over and over while he speaks. "When I woke up and saw my manager's car parked outside the tour bus, I went over there and found him like this." Jeremy opens the backdoor, revealing a gruesome sight I am unprepared to see.

A portly man in his sixties is curled up across the backseat, his eyes open and his full lips parted. He has bruising around his neck and his hands are bound in front with a zip tie. He is balding on top, with curly brown whisps of hair encircling his head like the halo I hope he has in his afterlife.

I shriek, covering my nose to smother the smell of death. "What is... Who is... Why did you... Is he really..."

None of my half-sentences make a lick of sense, so Carlos takes the wheel. "Did you call the police?"

Jeremy tilts his hand from side to side. "Sort of. I have an old friend who I think is still a cop. I was going to take the body to him, because he'll hear me out that I had nothing to do with this. I left a message for him, then stopped here on the way to see him."

Carlos' words come out slowly. "Why would someone assume you are guilty of murder? Finding a body in a car that isn't yours isn't exactly a smoking gun."

Jeremy grimaces. "People might think it's me who did this, because my manager and I had a pretty public fight."

Carlos sighs. "That's hardly a reason not to call the police first thing."

Jeremy shoves his hands in his pockets. "I'm on my way to my buddy Logan, who is a cop in Sweetwater Falls. I saw your sign, so I stopped here. I figure I might need representation. Sweetwater Falls doesn't have a law office." Jeremy casts Carlos a sheepish expression that I want to slap off his face. "Was that wrong?"

Carlos tugs out his phone. "Police first, representation if you need it *after* the police do their thing." He puts in a call to the Hamshire police, a hard look on his face.

My fingers are clumsy as I snap a picture on my phone and send it to the sheriff of Sweetwater Falls. I also send the picture to my boyfriend, Logan Flowers, who just so happens to be Jeremy's cop buddy.

I frown as I examine the body, my eyes drawn to the man's lips. "Is there something in his mouth?" I lean in to get a closer look, pointing at something white between the man's teeth. "What is that?"

Jeremy squints. "I don't know. I didn't notice it when I moved him."

Carlos' eyes close. "You moved the body?"

Jeremy grimaces. His neck shrinks as he offers up a guilty smile, like a boy who took a cookie from the cookie jar five minutes before dinner time. "Was that bad? He was in the driver's seat. I had to move him to drive the body here."

When Jeremy reaches out his hand toward the white

something stuck in the man's mouth, Carlos' voice turns sharp. "Don't touch anything. Leave it all for the police."

Carlos talks into his phone while Jeremy stands near the car with a hapless look on his face.

If Jeremy is back until they get to the bottom of who did this, then I want to solve this murder as quick as possible, so I can get Jeremy out of Sweetwater Falls and out of Marianne's life.

Read *Caramel Corruption* today!

Sign up to get alerts for New Releases at
www.MollyMapleMysteries.com

CHOCOLATE PEPPERMINT CUPCAKES

Yield: 12 cupcakes

From the cozy mystery novel *Peppermint Peril* by Molly Maple

"I love the look of the crushed candy canes sprinkled on the top of the peppermint frosting. The hot cocoa cupcakes add a dash of happiness to the kitchen as every surface is taken over by baked goods."

-Peppermint Peril

Ingredients for the Cupcake:
- ¾ cups all-purpose flour
- ½ cup unsweetened cocoa powder
- 1 tsp baking powder

½ tsp baking soda

½ tsp salt

1/3 cup vegetable oil

½ cup granulated sugar

2 large eggs, room temperature

2 tsp pure vanilla extract

½ cup plain yogurt or vanilla yogurt, room temperature

Instructions for the Cupcake:

1. Preheat the oven to 350°F and line a cupcake pan with cupcake liners.
2. In a medium bowl, sift together ¾ cups flour, 1 tsp baking powder, ½ tsp baking soda, and ½ tsp salt. Set flour mix aside.
3. In a large bowl, use a mixer to beat the vegetable oil and sugar on medium speed for three minutes. Beat until shiny, scraping down the sides of the bowl as needed.
4. Add eggs one at a time while the mixer runs on low speed. Add 2 tsp pure vanilla extract. Mix until smooth.
5. With the mixer on low speed, add the flour mixture in thirds, alternating with the yogurt. Mix to incorporate with each addition, scraping down the sides of the bowl as needed. Beat

until just combined. Batter should look a bit thin.

6. Divide the batter into your 12-count lined cupcake pan, filling each one 2/3 the way full.

7. Bake for 20-24 minutes at 350°F, or until a toothpick inserted in the center comes out clean.

8. Let them cool in the pan for 10 minutes, then transfer to a cooling rack. Cool to room temperature before frosting.

Ingredients for the Frosting:

2 sticks unsalted butter, softened

4 cups powdered sugar

2 tsp peppermint extract

¾ cup crushed candy cane pieces

Instructions for the Frosting:

1. Place 2 sticks unsalted butter into a stand mixer and beat until well combined.

2. Slowly add powdered sugar one cup at a time, alternating with peppermint extract until combined but not overmixed.

3. Mix in ¼ cup candy cane pieces. Beat until fluffy.

4. After frosting the cooled cupcakes, top with the remaining crushed candy cane pieces.

ABOUT THE AUTHOR

Author Molly Maple believes in the magic of hot tea and the romance of rainy days.

She is a fan of all desserts, but cupcakes have a special place in her heart. Molly spends her days searching for fresh air, and her evenings reading in front of a fireplace.

Molly Maple is a pen name for USA Today bestselling fantasy author Mary E. Twomey, and contemporary romance author Tuesday Embers.

Visit her online at www.MollyMapleMysteries.com. Sign up for her newsletter to be alerted when her next new release is coming.

Made in the USA
Las Vegas, NV
19 February 2022

44242916R00118